The Music
Business
(Explained In Plain English)

This book is dedicated to my parents, Avner and Frankie Naggar,
to my siblings, Mickey, Auri, Ron, and Tammy,
and to my nieces and nephews,
Jed, Sari, Josh, Danny, Elizabeth and Joe.

The Music Business

(Explained In Plain English)

WHAT EVERY ARTIST AND SONGWRITER
SHOULD KNOW
TO AVOID GETTING RIPPED OFF!

SECOND EDITION

DAVID NAGGAR, Esq.

© 2000-2004 David Naggar, Esq.
Second Edition. Fourth printing.

ISBN 1-57746-570-9

Library of Congress Catalog Number: 99-091713

Cover and book design by Gary Hustwit.
Cover photo by Ted Drake.

Published by DaJé Publishing, 1824 Beach Street, San Francisco, CA 94123.

Printed in the USA.

TABLE OF CONTENTS

ACKNOWLEDGMENTS

No book is written in a vacuum. I have learned a great deal from all of the materials mentioned in this book. Additionally, I would like to acknowledge the assistance I've received from people throughout the industry, including Jill Alofs of Total Clearance, Chris Barros of Winterland, Michael Cerchiai of Bimbos 365 Club, Tom Chauncey of the Rosebud Agency, Kevin Coloff of Paramount Pictures, David Conrad of Almo/Irving Music Publishing, Frank DuCharme of AFTRA, Dulce Farmer of Ellen Farmer Productions, David Gottlieb of the Cynthia Woods Mitchell Pavilion, Lyle Greenfield of Bang Music, Randy Grimmet of ASCAP, David Grossman of Paramount Pictures, Edward R. Hearn, Esq., Susan Heller, Esq., Herbie Herbert, David Hirshland, Esq. of Bug Music, Jim Kennedy, Esq. of ERHJK Publishing Administration, Jeff Leslie of EMI Distribution, Harry Poloner of EMI Music Publishing, George Scarlett of Tower Records, Ron Sobel of ASCAP, and Bruce Solar of Absolute Artists. Finally, a special thank you to Jeffrey Brandstetter. Without his work on the first edition, this book would not exist.

FORWARD TO THE SECOND EDITION

Much has changed in the music industry since the first edition of the Music Business (Explained In Plain English) was written. Music audiences and markets seem more fragmented than ever. Record companies have reexamined the way they "discover" and sign new artists; the number of new record labels is on the rise; there continues to be reshuffling of industry executives; and there has been a further consolidation of the major players in the industry. Further, copyright law has been modified; the internet explosion threatens to change, or liberate (depending on your view), the method of record distribution; and licensing of songs for use on the internet, on CD-ROM, and on DVD is adding new sources of income for songwriters and artists; the statutory mechanical royalty rates have continued to rise; artists grow increasingly sophisticated in merchandising; and global companies lay out huge sums of money just to get the right song in one of their commercials.

This updated and expanded edition covers these changes. As with the first edition of this book, I've made every effort to explain what you need to know in plain English.

INTRODUCTION

1. The Bottom Line

Music is art. This book is not about art!

There is a harsh reality about the music business that you probably already know: **People (not counting loved ones) will help you if they think your art will make them money. They will not help you if they do not think your art will make them money.**

Like other businesses, the multi-billion dollar music industry is driven by money. If you are new to the music business, or have been involved for years but never really had the "big picture" explained to you in plain English, this book is for you.

I have written it to help artists and songwriters understand the basics of this industry beyond the club scene. You don't need to know everything, but if you don't understand the basics, you are setting yourself up to be ripped off.

I've used a lot of footnotes because I am a lawyer and lawyers do that sort of thing. The information contained in the footnotes is important to clarify nuances, but is less important than the main text for an understanding of the "big picture." Also, I have tried to be specific about real numbers that are used in the industry, such as the royalty percentages earned by artists on record contracts and the royalty payment rate earned by songwriters for songs that appear on those records. Although I know these numbers are important to you, keep in mind that the numbers can change very quickly and many times over the course of your career. The concepts, however, remain the same and are the heart of the "big picture."

Let's get started...

2. SOURCES OF MUSIC INDUSTRY PROFITS

There are many different sources of profit for the musician and everyone else in the music business. Money is made from record sales, getting songs played on the radio, on television and in films, from concerts, the internet, CD-ROMs and DVDs, merchandising, advertising and more.

Today, for almost all performing artists, the real money flows first from making a record deal. In terms of money, successful record sales lead to everything else. The Recording Industry Association of America reports that record sales in the U.S. alone are close to 14 billion dollars annually. Global sales top 40 billion dollars. Of course, the *catch* to participating in this bonanza is getting a good record deal in the first place.

If, as an artist, you haven't created a *buzz* in the industry, it is extremely unlikely that you'll get a good record deal. No one will think that they can make money from your art, and no one will spend the resources on you to see to it that you have a money-making record.

If you are a songwriter, your real money flows mostly from getting your songs on records. If the artist (or artist's representative) doesn't think that putting your song on their record will ultimately make them more money than not having your song on their record, then it won't be on their record. Don't count on any exceptions to this.

Even though you may be both an artist and a songwriter, to follow the money flow, never confuse the terms "artist" and

"songwriter."

When I use the term "artist," I am talking about the person who performs the song, whether live or on a record, regardless of whether or not they wrote the song. When I use the term "songwriter," I am talking about the person who wrote the song, whether or not they perform it. Eric Clapton as an *artist* and Eric Clapton as a *songwriter* makes money in different ways for the performance of his songs (as an artist) and the writing of those same songs (as a songwriter).

Remembering this distinction is the most important key to understanding how you will make a living outside of the club scene in the music business.

BASICS FOR THE ARTIST

3. THE ARTIST'S BUSINESS ADVISORS

If you are an artist, there are three important advisors who will help you make key music business and career decisions: your personal manager, your attorney and your agent. There are good personal managers, attorneys and agents out there, but there seem to be many who are not. If you do not instinctively trust the person, do not deal with them.

The more high-powered, respected advisors you have on board, the more likely you are to get a record deal from a reputable record company.

SPECIFICS ABOUT YOUR PERSONAL MANAGER

The personal manager is the most important member of the three because if you get a good one, a record company is going to feel comfortable that there is someone keeping an eye on your music business life for you. The record company is then more likely to think that you will generate income — i.e., record sales — for them.

A good personal manager will advise you regarding all aspects of your career. They are responsible for promoting you, advising you about what songs to record, who to hire as your producer, who to sign a recording contract with, and when and where to tour. They also coordinate publicity campaigns and insulate you from time demands such as interview requests. The personal involvement each personal manager actually provides however, varies greatly.

The vast majority of personal managers receive between 15% and 20% of the artist's *gross* earnings as compensation. The percentage is negotiable, and depends not only on the extent of service that will be provided, but on the experience of the manager as well. In my view, it is worth hiring the best personal manager available, without regard to the exact percentage being paid. It is a better career move to part with 20% of gross earnings in order to hire a talented personal manager (one who can actively promote you and knows lots of people in the industry), rather than insisting on paying only 15% for someone who cannot further your career. When you become highly successful and the total dollars you earn grow wildly, you can then negotiate to lower the percentage a personal manager receives.

When negotiating with a manager, try to exclude from the definition of *gross* earnings on which he or she gets paid items which are not truly income, but rather are what I call "pass-throughs." Two example of this are (1)recording funds that the record company gave you, but that you used to pay the studio or other musicians, and (2)money given to you by the record company to help cover the cost of touring which you used to pay others. Your manager should not be paid on moneys that come to your account, but that you don't actually keep.

The term of a personal manager's contract is typically two to five years, but the term may be tied to album release dates or tour schedules, rather than to actual fixed calendar dates. Make sure that your contract with a personal manager states that he or she will be the person primarily representing you, rather than someone to whom the manager delegates responsibilities. Your contract should also include a provision allowing you to cancel the contract if, for example, you are not earning a certain amount by a given date, or have not received a record deal by a given date. Otherwise, you may be stuck for a long time with a personal manager who is taking you nowhere.

You should also be certain that the contract clearly states the amount of money your personal manager is to receive from earnings on deals you made *during* the term of the contract, but occurring *after* the expiration of the term. As an example, if you sign a deal to record five albums with Interscope Records, and soon thereafter have a falling out with your manager, should the manager receive 20% of all future profits? Clearly, that would not be fair, especially since your new manager will want 15% to 20% of your entire gross income no matter who else you are paying. Limit the percentage amount and length of time after the termination of the contract that the manager is to receive payment.

Here are some other critical questions you want to ask before you hire a manager:

1. Does he or she *really* like your music? Managing your music career is hard work. If you don't sense that your music is loved, the manager will inevitably work less hard.
2. Who does he or she know in the music industry? The more good relationships you can verify, the better.
3. How many other artists does he or she manage? In other words, how much time will he or she really have for you?

Surprisingly, some of the industry's top managers do not

have written contracts with their artists — just a handshake — and the only discussion point before hiring the manager is the percentage of your income the manager receives. All is left to good faith! While this may be a reality, it is *not* a good practice. As long as the relationship is going well, a handshake may be fine. But the moment things turn sour, you and your manager are likely to have very different ideas of what "the deal" was.

SPECIFICS ABOUT YOUR ATTORNEY

Attorneys specialize in different fields of the practice of law. A great corporate attorney may know absolutely nothing about the music business. It is important to hire an attorney who is knowledgeable specifically about the music business because attorneys in the music business are heavily involved in negotiating and structuring the deals artists make. There are so many hidden pitfalls buried in the contracts used in this industry, that hiring an attorney who understands the interplay between language and numbers is critical. One artist's 12% royalty on record sales may make the artist rich, while another artist's 12% royalty may pay that artist nothing.

As an artist, you must make sure you understand *in advance* how your attorney is going to charge you. Often, music attorneys use a retainer as a minimum payment against which they charge a flat hourly rate or "value" billing amount.[1] Expect to pay $200 an hour and up for a good music attorney in Los Angeles and New York, and a little less in Nashville, San Francisco, Miami, Atlanta and other major markets. Some

---

[1] With "value" billing, an attorney charges you based on their estimation of the value of the services rendered to you. If they did good work for you, they assign a value to it. This is not a great system for you, but it is what it is.

music attorneys, if they believe the artist will definitely be signed to a record deal, or the artist is already established, will forego a set fee in exchange for a percentage of the artist's earnings that flow from agreements the attorney negotiates on the artist's behalf (typically 5%). More and more, the most powerful attorneys in the industry insist on using this latter billing method. Obviously, it is to their advantage, not yours.

Here are some critical questions you want to ask before you hire an attorney:

1. Does he or she specialize in music law? If the answer is no, this may not be the right attorney for you, no matter how much you like them personally.

2. Who does he or she know in the music industry? Again, as with the personal manager, the more good relationships you can verify, the better. Access and trust will help get your record or publishing deal moving more quickly.

3. Who else does he or she represent? If the attorney has seen a lot of deals, he or she will know how much a record company will part with to make your deal. There is one matter, however, to be careful about. In the music industry, attorneys, or the firm at which an attorney works, often represent both record companies and artists. You don't want your attorney to negotiate a less favorable deal for you so that he can continue to do other legal work for the record company. The conflict of interest can be great, and has led to several lawsuits in the past few years.

SPECIFICS ABOUT YOUR AGENT

Music agents book concerts and other personal

appearances. But music agents are not as powerful as their counterparts in the film and television business. In some cases, particularly in country music, agents are completely bypassed. In any event, I suggest that you allow your personal manager to help guide you in your decision when picking an agent, because it is your personal manager who will be dealing with the agent most of the time.

Many agents agree to be bound by entertainment union contracts: AFM (American Federation of Musicians) contracts for musicians working as instrumentalists; and generally, AFTRA (American Federation of Television and Radio Artists) contracts for vocalists.[2]

These unions each have their own printed form contracts that agents and agencies use.[3] With few exceptions, these unions allow agents to charge only 10% of an artist's gross earnings in the areas in which the agent renders services. Therefore, agents do not get a portion of the artist's income from records sales, songwriting or publishing. (AFM and AFTRA's printed forms actually do have a place for the artist to initial that give agents earnings from records; *never* agree to this.) Some music agents are anxious for business and discount the percentage of the artist's gross income they receive to well below 10%. If an artist is generating major income from concerts, the fee from concert income may be as little as 4% to 5% (or even less if the agent really wants a big name act on their roster).

---

[2] Agents agree to be bound by other entertainment union contracts, as well: AEA (Actors' Equity Association) for stage performances, and SAG (Screen Actors Guild) for a vocalist's performance captured on film.

[3] If you sign with a major agency, they will have you sign agreements from all of the unions.

Generally, agents will want you to sign a contract that lasts for three years, but in some cases no contract is ever signed. As an artist, try to limit the term of the contract to one year if you have the negotiating strength. This will allow you to move on if your agent is not performing well. It will also allow you to renegotiate a lower fee if you are generating major dollars.

There are many important terms to negotiate before selecting an agent. Your attorney and personal manager can help you with these. For instance, the scope of the agency must be understood. Is your agent in charge of lining up all concerts and personal appearances, or something less? Also, the geographic territory in which the agent represents you, and the specific duties of the agent in obtaining and negotiating the terms of your engagements, must be agreed upon. Even more esoteric items, such as which union form governs when union forms overlap or contradict each other, must be negotiated. Make sure your attorney reviews the terms of your agency agreement. Otherwise, it could cost you a lot of money!

In addition to these three key advisors, when you actually have money coming in from a record or publishing deal, you will also need a business manager/accountant who is deeply familiar with the nuances of the music business. The business manager/accountant will be responsible for making sure that your tax situation is straight, will review royalty statements, assist in managing the financing of your tours, offer investment advice and manage your money. Since your attorney and personal manager will almost certainly be in place before you need a business manager, they will be able to guide you in picking a business manager.

4. SENDING OUT YOUR MATERIAL

Many artists make the mistake of sending their newly burned demo CDs to everyone they know *before* creating any local interest in their music and *before* having any of their business advisors in place. This is not an effective way of getting "discovered." At a cost of up to $1+ to make, package and send your demo, you would be better off playing the lottery.

Until you have music business advisors in place, your demo cannot be shopped to the powers at a major record company in earnest. First, create a "buzz" about your music; *then* have a business advisor shop your demo CD. The buzz is what will bring record industry people to hear you.

As an artist, material you send directly to an established record company will generally not be listened to, no matter how good it is. In part, this is because record companies fear potential liability in accepting material they have not asked for (what the industry calls "unsolicited" material). They do not want to be the target of a lawsuit by someone who later claims that their song was stolen and used by the record company.

Additionally, you should know that record companies receive more CDs than can properly be listened to. Therefore, the ones that actually do receive fair consideration are almost always received from professional managers or music attorneys who are known to the key people at the record company. These CDs are also of high quality (sonic quality, not necessarily good music).

You should also know that as the industry matures, most major labels are looking to sign artists who already have established record sales histories. They sign artists who have released their own CD to the public and have demonstrated an ability to generate local or regional sales without big label promotion. Like all businesses, record companies are looking to lower their risk. This risk averse attitude has been heightened in the wake of personnel cutbacks caused by internet piracy and lower sales.

Despite the advice I've offered above, if you choose to send out your own material directly to record companies, then at the very least, make sure that the material is "solicited,"[4] and send it to a particular named person in the Artists & Repertoire department of a record company (not "Attention: A & R director at Sony"). Send a CD with three to six songs on it. Make sure that your contact information is on the CD itself. Save the expense of sending lyric sheets and your press clippings,[5] but if you think your photographic image is a strong selling point (e.g., you are a drop dead hunk, drop dead gorgeous, or so bizarre you absolutely must be noticed) include it as well. Today, image can be as important as talent in generating record sales.

The only time that you, as an artist, will send your material to a publishing company is if you are also a songwriter. Publishing companies make money from owning rights to songs, not from signing artists. A major publishing company will

---

[4] It is better to telephone in advance even those people who will accept "unsolicited" material to ask if you can send them your music. Making it "solicited" gives your material a greater chance of being heard in the best light possible. Call to confirm that your demo CD has arrived, and follow up with a call a couple of weeks later to confirm that it has been listened to. Remember though, if you do send out your own material, it is extremely unlikely to get serious consideration.

[5] There are so many CDs received by A & R departments that most likely, lyric sheets and "puff" material will be separated from your CD well before it is listened to. If they like what they hear, they will ask for more.

not offer you (the *songwriter*) a publishing deal unless they are fairly certain that they can get you (the *artist*) a record deal, or unless they love your songs and you agree to have others record your songs. Once you've read this book, you will understand the economics of why that is. So, for an artist who is also a songwriter, the publishing deal often comes after the record deal is made.

If you want to be an artist, I recommend that you *not* sign a publishing deal until you are signed to a record deal, or until you are convinced that you will not be signed to a record deal without a publisher's help (i.e., if you have been rejected by the record companies you want to deal with or can't even get your foot in the door).

A list of names, addresses and key people in the A & R Departments of most every established record company can be found in the *Recording Industry Sourcebook*, which is available in bookstores.

5. RECORD COMPANIES, DISTRIBUTION, AND THE INTERNET

The record business is cyclical. It does well in good economic times, and poorly in bad times. In good economic times, record companies fight over artists and make deals that are better for the artists.

First, a couple of definitions: A "record" is defined in the industry as *any* device that can transmit sound, including CDs, tapes and videos. An "album" is usually defined as 8-12 selections (songs), with approximately 45 minutes of playing time.

RECORD COMPANIES

If an artist signs a recording contract with a record company, the artist will go into a studio and record songs for the record company. The record company then makes copies of the master recording (or subcontracts the making of copies to a manufacturing company) and ships these records to a *distributor*. The distributor is the wholesaler who sells the records to the retail stores (like Tower Records, Sam Goody or The Wherehouse). The record company then gears up its advertising, promotions, sales, etc., and voila, everyone is working together toward the artist's stardom.

I tend to categorize record companies into four groups: major label record companies, major label affiliate labels, independent labels (whose records are distributed through a major label) and true independent labels.

MAJOR LABEL RECORD COMPANIES

The biggest record companies are called "major label" record companies. Many of these companies, such as Arista, Atlantic, Capitol, Sony, and Virgin are identified in the pages that follow. Take a look at your collection of CDs and cassettes. The better known artists are usually represented by major labels, and the major label's name will appear prominently on the CD or cassette.

Many divisions of a major label record company are important to an artist's success. Although your record deal will be negotiated with the Business Affairs Department (home of the lawyers), the most important departments for your success are the A & R Department, the Marketing/Sales Department(s) and the Promotions Department.[6] **If you and your personal manager are friends with the key people in these departments, you are much more likely to be successful. As the legendary Joni Mitchell says, it's "stoking the star-maker machinery behind the popular song":**

1) The A & R Department

People in the A & R ("Artists & Repertoire") Department act as the "ears" of the record company. They are the ones charged with finding new artists and working creatively with them. However, just because an A & R person loves your music and helps you sign a deal with the record company does not mean that you are destined for stardom. Your record still has

---

[6] Not every major label record company has the same identical departments; nor do they identify the departments that serve particular functions by the same name as other major label record companies.

to be released, and it still has to sell. The path to glory is littered with artists who were already preparing themselves for stardom to strike after recording an album, only to discover that the record company decided not to release their album!

Understand that most of the people in the A & R Department of a major record company are not as important, in terms of deciding which artists get signed, as some would have you believe. Most of these people are under the age of 30 and are hired because they have convinced someone higher up in the company that they can spot and deliver talented artists to the record company.

The reality is that the dollar commitment a major label makes when they sign a new artist can be several hundred thousand dollars in recording costs, pressing and distribution, promotions, marketing, etc. A chief executive, such as Clive Davis at BMG, may hire someone to screen talented artists from the non-talented ones, but he and a few key advisors will be making most of the final decisions.

2) The Marketing and Sales Department(s)

These people are in charge of getting retail stores excited about carrying your record. They oversee album-cover artwork, promotional merchandise, advertising for your album, in-store displays and publicity.

3) The Promotions Department

The people in the Promotions Department are in charge of getting artists' records played on the radio. They do a lot of traveling and schmooze key radio station personnel to make sure your record gets played. If it doesn't get played, how is anyone going to know to buy it? The not-so-funny joke in the industry is, "How can you tell if a record is going to be a hit? Look at the promo budget."

♪ ♪ ♪

As I will discuss in the next subsection, major labels are either owned by, or are financially linked to, conglomerates which own the large distributors. These large distributors, in concert with major labels, have more power over record stores than independently owned distributors.

MAJOR LABEL AFFILIATE LABELS

Major labels often have special relationships with smaller labels whereby the major label may fund the smaller label's recording and operating costs in exchange for part of the smaller label's profits. The line between a major label affiliate label and an independent label whose records are not funded by a major label, but are distributed through them, is often blurred.

INDEPENDENT LABELS
(Whose Records Are Distributed Through A Major Label)

These record companies have few, if any, full-time employees. An independent label signs artists and sees to it that the records are recorded. Often, it contracts with a major label to perform the promotion, marketing and many other paper-intensive functions of a record company. Many major label distributed independents earn their keep simply by finding talented artists and making sure that the major label record company actively markets and promotes those artists.

TRUE INDEPENDENT LABELS

A true independent label has no association with a major label. Unlike major labels, major label affiliate labels and independent labels whose records are distributed through the major label network, true independents distribute their records through *independent distributors* not associated with the majors.

Which record company you choose to sign with is critical to your career. Do not go with the biggest just because it is the biggest. Your art may not get the full attention it needs to help you succeed. If the Marketing Department is busy pushing the Dixie Chicks, they may not have time for you. Meet with key members of the record company personnel who will be in charge of marketing and promoting your record before signing a deal. With an independent label, this may only be one person. Ask how they usually go about marketing and promoting an album. How committed are the key people to your album? Do they like your music? Will they push it even if it isn't initially successful? How much time and money are going to be spent marketing and promoting your album?

Remember, you will not be signed unless the people at the record company believe your art will make them money. It does help if they like your music because if the people you are working with at the record company think you will make them money but do not really like your music, they will drop you rather quickly from their roster if you do not make them money right away. Sadly, the short term profit motive is so strong at major labels and their affiliates, that even if they do like your music, you are likely to be dropped from their roster if you aren't a success right out of the box. And, if you are dropped, a stigma attaches, and it will be difficult to get signed by another major, ever. There are so many artists eager for a shot, that the label can churn talent in the hopes of finding an instant star, rather than developing one. If the industry operated twenty something years ago as it does now, Bruce Springsteen, whose first album wasn't so successful, would have been dropped and probably never heard from again.

Finally, when deciding which label to first sign with, keep in mind that each record company is unique, and each has its own strengths in different styles of music. Since the "scorecard" of who's who changes rapidly, the best way to know what services are offered by a particular record company is to ask (e.g., how they handle distribution, what resources are available to market and promote records, what previous success they've had getting radio airplay for artists who play your style of music).

THE DISTRIBUTION SYSTEM

For the most part, major retailers, such as Tower Records, will not carry an artist's record in their stores unless the record has a distributor. In any event, a strong distribution system is critical to ensuring that enough of your records are going to be found in enough places to sell enough copies to make money for everyone involved in the process of making and selling a record. A fairly large retail record store can physically carry only 60,000 to 70,000 total CDs, but there are many more CD titles than this in print. Even if the store carried only one copy of every CD title, not every CD could be in every store. In reality, there will be many copies of a popular CD at every retailer, which means that there is even less physical space for even a single copy of many CDs.

This fact leads to one of the biggest advantages of signing with a fully-staffed major label, if you can. As mentioned, major labels' records are distributed by large distributors, and large distributors are better able to get record stores to stock the labels' records. If a record store wants huge quantities of the latest Britney Spears record because it will sell and make money for the store, the distributor of Britney Spears' record, working in concert with one of its major labels, has power over the store and can "strongly suggest" that the store might like to give your record a chance as well.[7]

After years of consolidation, there are now only five "major" national wholesale distributors left in the U.S., and all of them are owned by conglomerates that own the major label record companies:

BMG (distributes Arista, BMG and RCA)[8]
EMI (distributes Capitol and Virgin)
Sony Music (distributes Columbia, Epic and Sony)
Universal Music Group (distributes Interscope, Island/Def Jam, and MCA)
WEA (distributes Atlantic, Elektra and Warner Bros.)

Even though so-called independent distributors such as

---

[7] Large distributors require large distribution networks. They actually have many more people working for them than a record company! As an example, Capitol Records has about 250 employees, but EMI, its distribution arm, has over 1200 employees. A few hundred of these employees are a part of EMI's manufacturing arm, but between 700 and 800 employees handle distribution.

[8] Each of these "major" distributors distribute records for many other record companies as well. *The Recording Industry Sourcebook* contains a current list of the distributed labels of each "major" distributor.

Caroline Records have become wholly owned by EMI and the other major conglomerates, there are still a variety of smaller national and regional independent distributors who are truly independent. Because contracts between distributors and the large retailers generally allow the retailers to return copies of records that do not sell, a distributor's cash flow can be erratic. All of the records a distributor thought they had sold to The Wherehouse or Sam Goody might come back to them a few months later. This is why some smaller independent distributors are constantly on the brink of financial failure. Others are not particularly reputable. For example, a decade ago, Tower Records had a vendor list of about 250 independent distributors. While some of the distributors merged operations, the vast majority simply went out of business. Today, Tower has winnowed its vendor list to 80 vendors.

If you are considering selling your own CD or tape through an independent distributor, make sure the distributor is in sound financial condition. Here's an oversimplified example of what might be specified in the contracts between (1)you and the distributor, and (2)the distributor and the retailer, that explains why you need to be concerned: Suppose you "sell" your records to the distributor on January 15. Your contract with the distributor is likely to state that the distributor must pay you sometime in April. In the meantime, the distributor "sells" your records to Tower Records, for example. The distributor's contract with Tower will state that Tower must pay for your records sometime before the end of March (i.e., before the April date the distributor agreed to pay you). So far, so good.

But remember that in the music industry most contracts between a retailer and a distributor allow the retailer the right to return to the distributor any record that the distributor previously "sold" to the retailer that the public didn't buy.[9] If Tower decided in March to return to your distributor two thousand records of other artists which it could not sell to the public, but for which it already paid the distributor in December of last year, then the distributor owes a refund to Tower on those two thousand records. Even if Tower actually sold all one thousand of your records to the public, since two thousand is more than one thousand, your distributor actually owes Tower money, not the other way around. By April, the distributor will also owe you money for your one thousand records that were sold. You have been out of pocket the cost of making the CDs and tapes since January 15, but, by the end of April, you may find that the distributor has paid for its own salaries and overhead but has no money left over to pay you. The moral is: check the distributor's financial statement before signing a contract with them!

Although it is usually better to have a major distributor distributing your records, depending on the style of your music or where you expect it to sell, this may not always be the case (assuming the independent is financially sound).

Independent distributors have less power over record stores, and frankly sometimes serve as a weigh station for smaller labels and artists who are on their way up (or on their way down). Nevertheless, independent distributors, such as City Hall, may serve your art better than a major distributor. For example, independent distributors are significant players in distributing rap, hip-hop, and newer styles of underground music. Also, because they are typically less bureaucratic, they can get product

---

[9] A new record from a major label may stay in the store for 90-150 days before it will be returned to the distributor as unsold.

into their system and solicit orders more quickly than a major label record/distribution company can.

A traditional distribution entity (major distributors and independent distributors) buys from manufacturers (i.e., record companies) and sells directly to retail stores. These distributors also sell records to sub-distributors known as "One Stops" and "Rack Jobbers" who have niche markets:

ONE STOPS

One Stops carry records from many record companies; hence, "one stop" shopping for the retailers who wish to purchase these records. One Stops sell records used in jukeboxes, and also sell to "Mom and Pop" retailers in small quantities. The markup to "Mom and Pop" retailers is generally higher than it is to chain stores such as Sam Goody or The Wherehouse.

RACK JOBBERS

Rack Jobbers buy records from traditional distributors, and then sell the records in leased floor space within major superstores such as Wal-Mart and K-Mart. When you buy a record at Wal-Mart, you aren't really buying it from Wal-Mart.

Record companies also license others to sell the record company's records to consumers, thereby bypassing the traditional distributor. Examples of such licensees are: (1)record clubs, (e.g., Columbia House and BMG Music Services -- buy 1, get 11 free); and (2)television packagers (e.g., Perry Como's Christmas Album, K-tel).

DISTRIBUTION THROUGH THE INTERNET

Record labels and well known artists are increasingly using the internet to distribute records directly to music fans. (They are also feverishly fighting to limit and control digital piracy through lawsuits and by sponsoring legislation. Napster is now legit. Free file sharing sites such as KaZaa and Morpheus are under fire). Since the whole point of distribution is to get records to places where the customer can make a purchase, many people view the internet as the great equalizer which will take power away from the major labels and their distribution dominance. Any artist can place his or her record in a virtual store such as Amazon.com or on an MP3 site, and their fans can then purchase a hard copy or just download the music. The record is always available to everyone with internet access.

The challenge for the unknown artist, from a business point of view, is to alert enough people that the artist actually has a product worth purchasing. In my view, the new internet reality won't disrupt the dominance of the majors. The internet is full of clutter, and the artist still needs to differentiate him or herself from everyone else who places their CD on the internet. Without the muscle of record labels to arrange media publicity, promote radio and webcasting airplay, and obtain prominent placement in record and cyberstores, a major independent internet sales breakthrough will likely be the exception, not the rule. More likely, if an independent artist's internet sales show promise, a major label will then step in and offer the artist the major promotion dollars necessary to take the record to the next level.

♪ ♪ ♪

Let's discuss how an artist makes money from records.

6. ARTIST ROYALTY RATES AND PAYMENT CALCULATIONS

The most important contract in the entire music industry is the record contract. For making a record, an artist gets paid a portion of the money the record company takes in from record sales. This amount, which is negotiated between the record company and the artist, is known as the artist's royalty.

Having a basic understanding of the way in which royalty payments are calculated is critical if you are to understand the amount of money an artist can make from a record. In negotiating a record deal, an attorney who is familiar with the nuances of the music business and has a good sense of numbers really helps because, as I stated earlier, one artist's 12% royalty may make him or her rich, whereas another artist's 12% royalty may yield them nothing.

A record company, through its distributor, may sell a CD with the *suggested retail list price* of the record ("SRLP") of $17.98 to a retailer for about $11.40. The distributor takes a cut of 10%-14% of the $11.40.

Even though the record company receives only about half of $17.98 (true independents typically receive less than half), most major record company contracts state the artist's royalty rate as a percentage of the SRLP (of $17.98), not as a percentage of the wholesale price they receive.

Here are some typical artist royalty rates. The actual royalty rate, of course, will depend on the artist's negotiating strength. *These royalty rates are the "base rates," and in many record contracts the rates are lowered if certain criteria are not met:*[10] Note, for example, that for everyone but the most successful artists, the stated "base rates" are usually reduced by 15% to 20% for sales of CDs.

For a new artist who has never had a record deal, or a signed artist who has never sold more than say 100,000 albums of any record, a typical royalty rate will be 12% to 14% of the SRLP if he or she is signed to a major label record company. The spread is a bit wider if signed to an independent label. The typical range for an independent label is 10% to 14% of SRLP.[11]

An established artist whose last album sold 200,000 to 500,000 copies is likely to be able to negotiate a royalty rate of 14% to 16% of the SRLP.

A major star whose last album sold 750,000 copies or more can expect to command a royalty rate of 16% to 18% of the SRLP.

---

[10] Generally, the major labels apply the base rate only to records sold: (1)at full price; (2)in the U.S.; (3)on their main label (many majors own subsidiary labels and this can affect royalty payments); (4)through retail record stores; and (5)through a record company's normal distribution channels. Royalty rates for the same record are different depending on the method of distribution! Various types of reduced royalty rates are discussed in Chapter 7, "Other Artist Royalty Rates."

[11] A few record companies, mostly smaller ones, calculate royalties as a percentage of the wholesale price they receive from the distributor. If this is the case in your record deal, the stated royalty percentages should be roughly double the royalty rate of the standard SRLP royalty rate that is discussed above. This is because the actual dollar payment to the artist who has an SRLP royalty rate of 10% (of $17.98), is the same to the one who has a wholesale royalty rate of 20% (of $8.99).

Royalties for "singles" rarely exceed 12% to 14%, and new artists are not likely to get even 10% of the SRLP unless a bidding war for their services breaks out.[12]

As you can see, the more sales the record company expects to generate from an artist's record, the higher the percentage they will be willing to pay the artist. Also, an escalated percentage of the SRLP on each individual album can be negotiated. For instance, the artist may receive only 12% on the sale of the first 100,000 units, 14% on the sale of the next 200,000 units and 16% on sales of units in excess of 300,000.

Now that you know the general royalty rate percentages various artists receive, you must understand that an artist doesn't actually get paid on their full royalty rate. By way of example, an artist with a CD royalty rate of say 12% of the SRLP will not actually get paid 12% of $17.98 ($2.16) for each CD sold. An artist's royalties from a gold album (i.e., one selling 500,000 copies) will definitely not generate $1,080,000 ($500,000 x $2.16) in artist's royalties. Not even close.

There are many deductions from the $1,080,000 found in every record company contract. But, the types of deductions, and the amount of those deductions, that each record company has in its form contract are not the same. And contracts do change. As I write this, BMG is planning to overhaul its contract to remove some deductions, and pay royalties on wholesale prices rather than on SRLP. In all of these contracts, the deductions must be reviewed carefully. Let's look at some of the typical ones.

---

[12] Some companies use what is called an "up-lift" (130% of the wholesale price), instead of the SRLP, as the retail price on which they base the artist's royalty rate. This usually serves to reduce the royalty payment actually received by the artist!

A REAL WORLD EXAMPLE OF A ROYALTY PAYMENT CALCULATION

(This stuff is a little dense. Alright, maybe more than a little dense, but it's important that you have an understanding of how this works.)

To start with, the record company will deduct a "packaging charge" off the top of the SRLP, from which the artist gets no royalty. Typically, the deduction is as follows:

10% deduction on vinyl records (now hardly
   relevant);
20% deduction for cassettes;
25% for CDs.

Notice that the packaging deduction for CDs is fully 5% more than the packaging deduction charged for cassettes. There is no economic justification for this.

Here's the step-by-step math for calculating CD royalties:

SRLP of the CD	$17.98
Less: Packaging (25% of $17.98)	− $ 4.50
	$13.48

So, if for example, an artist's royalty "base rate" is 15%, a 20% reduction for CD sales would leave the artist with a royalty rate of 12% of the SRLP for CD sales. The artist's royalty would be $1.62 per CD (12% of $13.48; not 12% of $17.98).

Most often, the artist's royalty rates are called "all-in," which means that the artist is responsible for paying his or her record producer out of the artist's share of royalties. Typically, the producer receives a royalty of 3% to 4% of the SRLP. Therefore, if the artist has to pay the producer his or her share from the artist's share (e.g., artist's share of 12% less 3% to the producer), the artist's remaining share is only 9% of $13.48 ($1.21).

Also, "sold" is defined in an unusual way in the record business. Often, it turns out to be only 85% of records actually sold, so the artist actually receives only $1.21 on 85 of every 100 CDs sold.[13] The artist gets no money on 15 of every 100 CDs sold!

Continuing with the math:

Assume 200,000 CDs are shipped to the stores:	200,000
Times: Royalty per CD that goes to the artist	x $1.21
Times: Royalty-bearing percentage	x 85%
Gross Royalty to the artist	$205,700.00

When calculating the amount of royalties to actually pay the artist, the record company withholds a part of what it may owe the artist. (That's right, you don't get the $205,700 yet.) They do so because contracts between distributors and record stores generally allow records "sold" by the distributor to the store to be returned to the distributor if the public isn't buying the record. Distributors receive the same type of return privilege from record companies.

---

[13] This is because most record companies historically have given retailers "free goods." While a few record companies may call their "free goods" by another name, they still only consider 85% of records really sold to be counted as "sold."

This is important to you as the artist because *all* of your records can be returned if the public isn't buying them! The record companies and distributors argue that they do not know which records will come back to them even though computer tracking makes this less true today than ever before.

The money the record company holds back and does not pay the artist because of this return privilege is called a ***reserve***. Reserves may be held for as long as two years before they are finally paid to the artist.

Typically, a record company withholds paying an artist 25% to 40% of the royalties that would otherwise be due to an artist if the record store's purchase of the artist's CD or tape from the record company was final. The exact percentage is negotiable and depends on the artist's previous record sales track record. For rock artists and newer artists, a reserve of 30% to 40% is more common because a seemingly hot rock star's album may go cold in a hurry, and the record sales that a new artist can generate are unknown.

Continuing with the example of royalty payments from the previous pages:

Gross Royalty (from above)	$205,700.00
Less: 30% reserve (typical of a moderately successful rock artist)	− $ 61,710.00
	$143,990.00

As an artist, you may never see any of the $205,700, let alone the $143,990, because of ***advances*** and ***recoupment*** of advances.

Here's how advances and recoupment work: A record company often pays out money to the artist, or on the artist's behalf, before records are sold and royalties are earned. This is called an **advance**. For instance, the cost of going into the studio and recording the record is treated by the record company as an advance payment of record royalties to you. An advance is not only monies paid directly to the artist; it is also monies paid on the artist's behalf to the studio where the record is made, the producer and studio musicians. In addition, typically 50% of the cost of "independent" promoters (i.e., people hired by the record company who aren't employees of the record company but are hired to schmooze with radio station personnel so that your song receives radio airplay) and 50% of the cost of making the video will be considered to be advances against record sales. Also, if the record company helps pay for part of the cost of your tour, most likely all of this cost will be considered an advance against the record sales. In some record contracts, the items considered "advanced" are painstakingly listed and can be a page long.

Typical recording cost dollar amounts advanced by a record company are as follows:

New artist signed to an independent record company
— $0 to $80,000
New artist signed to a major label record company
— $150,000 to $400,000
A moderately successful artist — $250,000 to $500,000
Major star — $750,000 or more[14]

Independent promotion, inexpensive videos and tour support can easily run another $150,000 to $200,000. When money is made from selling a record, the record company keeps all of the artist's royalties to pay itself back before the artist gets paid anything. This is called ___recoupment___. The record company is recouping what it advanced the artist, and this may mean that the artist never actually receives any royalties from the record company, unless the artist's record is very successful.

In our example, if the record company advances $200,000 to cover the costs of recording, and another $150,000 to cover the cost of some independent promotion, or to help underwrite the cost of a tour, the artist owes the record company $206,010 ($350,000 less $143,990), assuming the 30% reserve of the records "sold" to the record stores go unsold to the public and are eventually returned to the record company.

Not everything the record company pays for, however, is an advance. If the artist has negotiated his or her contract well, the following are not typically charged to the artist's account as an advance by the record company: manufacturing and shipping costs of a record, Marketing/Sales Department(s) expenses and Promotions Department expenses.

In addition, there are a few other deductions from the amount actually paid to the artist. While all deductions should be reviewed with your attorney before you sign any contract with a record company, the biggest ones you should be aware of are that no royalty payments are made on either (1)real free goods,

---

14 Often, when the artist has signed a record contract to record multiple albums, the advance to the artist for making any album other than the first one is stated as a percentage of the royalties earned from the artist's previous album. However, there is usually a minimum and a maximum that the record company will be obligated to advance irrespective of the actual sales of the previous album. The minimum protects the artist from a small advance if the previous album was a bomb, and the maximum protects the record company from paying a huge advance if the artist's previous album sells millions and millions of copies.

or (2)promotional copies of records.

Real free goods are records given away by a record company to retailers as an incentive to get them to carry more of a particular record the record company is trying to push.

Promotional copies are given free by the record companies to radio stations and others in the industry who help promote records. They are not supposed to be for sale, but unfortunately, promotional copies often end up being sold.

If the royalty earned by the artist doesn't cover the amount of the advance (this actually happens a lot), the artist is said to be "in the red" and has a deficit. This amount is typically carried over to the next record through what is called *cross-collateralization*, which means that the artist won't see any of his or her royalties earned as an artist from the next record (even if it is a hit) until the deficit from the first record is paid back to the record company in full. If there isn't a second record, the record company generally swallows the loss and the artist is no longer responsible for it.

If you are an artist and a songwriter, never allow the royalty payments due you as an artist from your record deal to be cross-collateralized with royalty payments due you as a songwriter for having written the songs on the album. (Royalties earned as a songwriter will be discussed in the next part of this book, which is about songwriter basics.)

So how much of a royalty does an artist make on a gold album? (Remember, a gold album is one which sells 500,000 copies.):

CD (suggested retail price)	$	17.98
Less: Packaging (25%)	− $	4.50
	$	13.48
Times: Net royalty rate to artist		
(12% "all-in" less 3% to producer)	x	9%
Gross Royalty per CD (9% of $13.48)	$	1.21
Times: 500,000 albums	x	500,000
SUBTOTAL		$605,000.00
Times: Royalty-bearing percentage	x	85%
Gross Royalty		$514,250.00
Less: Typical recording costs and other		
promo/video/touring/ advances		
(some paid to the artist)[15]		− $350,000.00
TOTAL ROYALTY TO THE ARTIST		$164,250.00

♪ ♪ ♪

Not as much as you thought, eh? Note that because reserves are typically 25% to 40%, the artist will get only a fraction of the $164,250 until perhaps two years later. And the amount of the total deductions may be much higher. The point is, even a gold album could easily leave an artist in the red, owing money to the record company. A high royalty rate may be something people like to brag about at cocktail parties, but stated royalty rates are only part of the equation and can be misleading. If you are reviewing proposals from several record companies, compare the bottom line dollars going into your pocket. Do not be fooled

---

[15] Recording funds advanced to an artist to cover recording costs which are not spent are kept by the artist. But don't count on much money being left over unless you are a major star with a major budget.

into focusing on the royalty rate itself.[16]

One final important point about the money that the artist actually gets to keep: the record producer's royalties are calculated somewhat differently. Remember, the producer's royalties are paid out of the artist's share of royalties. Traditionally, producer contracts state that the producer is not entitled to payment of his or her share of the SRLP until the artist's recording costs have been recouped by the record company. However, once the artist's recording costs have been recouped, the producer's royalties are owed immediately and must be actually paid to the producer for every record then sold.

In other words, if a record company was fully recouped when the sales of an album reached 300,000, the artist would finally actually receive money (the artist's percentage of the SRLP) on the next album sold. But when that album is sold, the producer is entitled to receive his or her share of the SRLP on all 300,001 albums sold! Because of this anomaly, and because the artist may still be in the red from a previous record (due to cross-collateralization), the artist can be responsible for paying the producer a lot of money even though the record company doesn't owe the artist a penny. **It is, therefore, generally a good idea to insist that the record company be responsible for paying producer royalties in the event of a shortfall.**[17]

---

[16] Royalty rates are often structured in ways that are much more complicated than the example above, but the principles are the same. For instance, many royalty rates are based on the sales of the previous album or on the average sales of previous albums. Also, the stated royalty rate for any given album may increase when certain levels of sales are achieved. For instance, the royalty rate might be 12% of SRLP for the first 100,000 albums sold, 13% of SRLP for the next 100,000 albums sold, 14% of SRLP for the next 100,000 albums sold, and so on.

Just so you know, many record companies will dictate to a lesser established artist who his or her record producer will be. Often, a record company chooses a producer based on how much the producer's "name" will help with marketing.

Typical advances for producers are as follows: Those working on an album with a budget of $150,000 expect to receive advances of $3,000 per master for each cut on the album (e.g., $30,000 per album if there are 10 songs on the album). Sought-after producers working on an album with a larger budget expect a much larger advance, as much as $10,000 per master or more. In addition, sometimes a separate "mixing fee" of $3,000 per master must be paid to the person who performs the final mix-down, blending the many tracks of a recording project down to two-track stereo, regardless of whether they are also the producer.

Many major label record companies are now directly advancing to the producer a portion of the recording costs that used to be advanced to the artist. This is especially true if the producer has his or her own studio. Even in this scenario, the money advanced to the producer is still "recoupable" from the artist's royalties before the artist sees a penny from record sales.

As I mentioned earlier, an artist's royalty rate on the same record varies depending on methods of distribution and

---

[17] Of course, the record company will extract other concessions for agreeing to do this, and will add the money it pays the producer to the amount "advanced" to the artist. Other than as noted above, and in this footnote, producer royalties are generally calculated in the same way as artist royalties. The exception to this is for video sales. In that instance, the producer gets half of the customary royalty (on the theory that the audio — as opposed to the video — portion of the master is only half of the product).

sale. A more thorough list of the various royalty rates an artist receives is included in the next section.

But before I turn to other royalty rates, know that the whole royalty rate structure seems to be teetering. In the last few years two factors have led to many attempts, even from major labels, to simplify royalty payment calculations: First, the word is out on how these contracts work, so why go through the complications. Additionally, legal downloads of music through the internet (ipods, etc.) are finally taking off, making certain deductions and royalty payment models seem outdated.

For example, since the 1960's, "singles" haven't made much money for record companies and so a lower royalty rate was paid out to artists (often about 3/4 of the album royalty rate). In part, the failure of singles to make money was due to the higher relative costs of packaging, placing and promoting singles. But there are no packaging costs on the internet, and as downloads of singles explode, they become a profit center for the majors. Today as I write this, internet sales still account for fewer that 2% of industry sales, but sales are expected to grow quite rapidly.

That is why top attorneys now insist that major labels apply the same percentage royalty rate payable on singles downloaded from the internet as are payable on album sales. This only makes sense. On the other hand, you might find it strange that the record companies are still able to charge packaging deductions for downloads. Bear in mind that all deductions are just a means of getting to a bottom line profit number. Eliminating this deduction might in turn lead to a renegotiated royalty rate itself. But, as I say, all is in flux as the music business goes through an overhaul to accommodate the effects of the internet.

7. OTHER ARTIST ROYALTY RATES

Actual payment to the artist of the following royalties is subject to the same deductions discussed in the previous section.

1) MID-LINE RECORDS

After the record has had its initial run in the current release and is no longer being actively promoted by the record company, it becomes what is called a *catalog item*. Typically, catalog items are sold to retailers at a reduced SRLP (60% to 80% of top-line new release records--thus, mid-line). A record that is a catalog item, or is otherwise sold by the record company to retailers at a reduced 60% to 80% price, carries a reduced royalty payment (typically 66-2/3% to 75% of the artist's base rate discussed in the previous section).

2) BUDGET RECORDS

These records are sold to retailers at an even more reduced SRLP. You see them selling at the store for less than 60% of the price of top-line new release records. The artist's royalty rate on budget records is typically 50% of the base rate.

3) CUTOUTS AND DELETES

Cutouts and deletes are records taken out of the record company catalog because the record is *really* dead. Artists get no royalties for these. They are being sold at a loss. These are the records in the junk bins of record stores that we've all thumbed through, hoping to find a great buy.

4) RECORD CLUBS

A record company contract will state that the record company has the exclusive right to "license" the recordings an artist makes for them. This means that if anyone wishes to use the recording, they must pay the record company a fee for the privilege. Record clubs pay record companies such a fee. Typically, the royalty rate received by the artist for records sold by the record club is 50% of the artist's base rate, but there is usually a cap on the total royalty payment such that the record company never has to pay the artist more than 50% of the actual licensing fee the record company receives from the record club. There are also substantial reductions in royalty payments owed to the artist for any of his or her albums which are given free to the record club by the record company. Record company "freebies" can equal the total number of albums of all artists sold by the record company to the record club. This means that a particular artist can get burned if the record company designates all of his or her albums to be freebies.

5) COUPLING AND COMPILATIONS

Coupling occurs when two or more artists appear on the same album. When many artists appear on the same album, the album is sometimes called a compilation album. The total royalties generated by such albums are split among the artists.

6) SAMPLERS

Samplers are a form of coupling. Generally, they are low-priced albums in which a few new artists are featured. Often, there is no royalty payment because these records are sold by record companies as promotions.

7) PREMIUMS

These are records sold in conjunction with other products, such as cereal. The royalty rate is typically 50% of the base rate, but the rate is not a percentage of the SRLP; rather, it is a percentage of the actual price at which the record is sold to the advertiser. The artist should try to limit this type of record sale from occurring without the artist's consent.

8) FILM SOUNDTRACK ALBUM

The artist's record company may grant a film company a license to use the record company's artist's performance of a song in the film company's soundtrack album. The artist's royalty rate is usually 50% of the record company's licensing fee.

9) HOME VIDEO SALES

Generally, the royalty rate is 10% of the wholesale price of the video.

10) GREATEST HITS ALBUM

An artist's royalties for a "Greatest Hits" album are based on a blended rate of the royalty rates the artist received from the albums on which each song first appeared.

11) FOREIGN ROYALTIES

These vary widely depending on the artist's recognition in a particular country. In Canada, the royalty rate is typically 85% of the base rate. In industrialized nations such as the

United Kingdom, France, Italy, Germany, Japan and Australia, the royalty rate is typically 60% to 75% of the base rate. In what is referred to in a typical record contract as "Rest of World," the royalty rate is typically 50% to 60% of the base rate.

12) PUBLIC PERFORMANCE OF MASTER

In many foreign countries, money is paid by radio stations to the record company for playing the record. Radio stations in the U.S. do not make such payments to the record company (but webcasters must!). U.S.-based record companies have typically refused to pay the artist any additional royalties for foreign performances, although with the growth of the international market, requiring payment for these performances is increasingly becoming worth fighting for.

13) MASTER USE LICENSE

Royalties are received by record companies from licensing the use of a recording in film, television, advertisement, the internet, CD-ROM and DVD. Record companies typically pay the artist 50% of the money earned.

14) DIGITAL PERFORMANCE RIGHT IN SOUND RECORDINGS ACT OF 1995 AND THE DIGITAL MILLENNIUM COPYRIGHT ACT

The copyright owner of your master recording, typically the record company, also has a right in certain cases to receive royalties when the record is digitally transmitted. This includes the right to receive royalties from webcasters. In 2002, new law effectively mandates that certain webcasters pay set royalty rates to record companies (e.g., commercial internet radio stations must pay 7/100th of a cent per song per listener to the owner of the master). While, at present, the income generated as a result of digital transmission laws is not great, make sure your record contract calls for you to receive a royalty payment equal to 50% of the money earned by the record company from any new source of income the record company receives, unless another royalty rate is specifically set by legal statute.

Record companies also receive payment for legal downloads of songs. With so many "free" sites on the internet, pay sites haven't worked so well. But the combination of record industry lawsuits, and Apple's ipod have begun to turn things around. Record labels are still looking for the right pricing formula to maximize profits from the internet and this is likely to play out over years. For now, make every effort to have the major label apply the same percentage royalty rate payable on your singles downloaded from the internet as are payable on your regular retail store album sales. Unfortunately, most pre-internet contracts didn't contemplate the revival of singles as a profit center, so artists with these older contracts are generally paid royalties on sales of internet singles at a reduced rate.

Digital transmission will become a *much* larger percentage of the music business. It eliminates many inefficiencies in the industry, including the cost of manufacturing copies of CDs that may not sell, the cost of shipping CDs across the country, and the business transaction cost associated with the record stores having the right to return unsold product to record companies. Because new unforeseen sources of artist royalty income are inevitable from the digital revolution (e.g., ringtones for cell phones), in this time of transition in the music business, make sure your lawyer covers future looking royalty opportunities.

8. KEY RECORD CONTRACT DEAL POINTS

Now that you have a sense of the royalty numbers, the key points of a record contract discussed below will make more sense to you. They all deal, to one extent or another, with whether money ends up in the artist's pocket, or in the record company's pocket. To discuss each at length would make this book far too long and would probably bore you to death. Also, I have not discussed issues regarding your creative freedom and control. These you already know enough about to negotiate wisely. Keep this list as a handy reference for when you are negotiating or renegotiating your record deal. Make sure you discuss each point with a good lawyer.

1) ROYALTY RATES AND CALCULATIONS

As previously mentioned, an artist makes money from the record company by receiving royalties from the record company. The more records you sell, the higher your royalty should be. Hopefully, I have given you a good understanding of how this works. Do carefully review any provision which calls for reduced royalty rates on "new format" records. Inevitably, there will be a format which replaces the CD as the most popular way to hear music, whether it is DVD, or a yet to be discovered format.

2) LENGTH OF CONTRACT/OPTIONS

Generally, major labels insist that a new artist sign a contract that lasts nine months after the artist has delivered one completed album. Major label record companies also insist on receiving anywhere from three to nine consecutive "options" to extend the term of the contract. As an artist, these options may require you to make many albums at a reduced royalty rate. Every effort should be made to limit the number of options the record company has to extend the term of your contract to four or less. The original contract should contain a clause that states the royalty payments due for each album recorded under subsequent option periods. The artist's attorney should negotiate for higher royalty rates for each new album recorded.

3) RELEASE OF THE RECORD

Just because an artist signs a record deal and makes an album does not mean that the album will be released or distributed, unless the artist negotiates this into his or her contract with the record company. The release of the album should be guaranteed by the record company, or, at the very least, the contract should allow the artist to go elsewhere if the album is not released. Also, in the case of a major label, the album should be released on the record company's main label, not some smaller label they just acquired or are starting.

4) PROMOTION, MARKETING & INITIAL RUN OF THE RECORD

It is critical that your record receives adequate promotion or it will die. You should attempt to get the record company to commit to a certain dollar amount that will be expended on the promotion of your records to radio stations, and on the marketing of your records to stores (traditional resellers and internet). If they will not do so, you must question their commitment to you. Additionally, if there is a bidding war for your services, you should attempt to get the record company to commit to hire "independent promotion" people on your behalf. These people are well-connected with radio station programmers, but are not part of the record company's Promotions Department. You also want to limit how much of what a record company pays to an independent promoter is recoupable by the record company. Finally, the initial run of the record (before a record company is allowed to make the record a mid-line item) should be at least twelve months.

5) TOUR SUPPORT

Record companies want you to tour because doing so sells records. Many tours are actually money losers. I discuss this in greater detail in Chapter 19, "On Tour." If your tour is a money loser, generally 100% of the costs advanced by the record company for the tour are recoupable by the record company. Try to get the record company to guarantee tour support, at least for your first tour.

6) MERCHANDISING

Many record companies want the right to sell merchandise (t-shirts, cups) with your likeness or logo on it. If you grant them this right (either directly, or through one of their affiliates), make sure that you actually get paid a royalty from the sale of merchandise, and that your share of the profits are not used to offset any loss they claim you have from record sales. I discuss this in greater detail in Chapter 20, "Selling Merchandise."

7) VIDEOS

Provisions in record contracts regarding music videos are growing in length as the importance of videos to music industry profits grows. Today, music videos themselves are money losers, but having a video is increasingly important to achieving high record sales. If you enter into a deal with a major label, it is imperative that the label provide the funds to make the video. Typically, a record company will agree to charge only 50% of the cost of making a video as recoupable against the audio (i.e., the record), but they will charge 100% of the cost of making a video as recoupable against the sales of videos, should there be any.

8) LIMITATIONS ON COUPLING AND COMPILATIONS

Try to limit the record company's ability to force you to participate in these arrangements. They may be good for the record company in the short run and bad for your career in the long run. *You* should have final control over your image, not the record company.

9) LIMITS ON MULTI-MEDIA EXPLOITATION

Try to limit the record company's ability to license your performances without your approval. Whether its on the Web or in the movies, you want final control over your art and image.

10) ALBUM COVER ARTWORK

Speaking of image, who controls the album artwork is negotiable. This can be important not only for your image, but also in determining whether you or the record company profits from merchandising associated with the artwork.

11) TERRITORY

For less established artists, a record company's "territory" is usually defined as the entire "universe." This means that the record company can sell your records anywhere. You may wish to limit a record company's territory if they are unable to effectively market your album somewhere. For instance, if you expect your music to be especially popular in Japan, it is important that the record company which sells your music in Japan can do so effectively. As more and more records are sold outside of the U.S. and Canada, the extent of a record company's territory is apt to be negotiated more heavily in the future.

12) RESERVE LIMITATIONS

Try to negotiate the "reserve" percentage down as best you can. Also, try to limit the amount of time a record company can hold on to the reserve once it knows that your records were actually sold to the general public. With the widespread use of Soundscan®, which tracks record sales by scanning the UPC code on the back of each record, the record companies have a pretty good idea of which albums are selling. If your records have already sold, the reserve should be reduced accordingly.

13) CONTROLLED COMPOSITION CLAUSE

In a typical record contract, the money you earn for writing songs that appear on a record is reduced if you are the artist on the record. This limitation is contained in the *controlled composition* clause of a record contract. I will explain this clause in the next part of this book. You need to understand how songwriters get paid in order to understand it. For now, know that it is a critically important part of the artist's record deal.

14) OWNERSHIP OF THE MASTERS

Ownership of your master recordings allows the record

company to exploit them. Hence their war against "free" websites. If you are a major star you can probably insist on some type of reversion to you at some point in the future. But if you are a new artist, you never know if, or when, the record company might drop you from their roster. Try to negotiate to obtain ownership of all of the masters you recorded, whether they made it on an album or not. This way, should you be dropped from the label, you can exploit them, or, at the very least, not be haunted by them when the record company that dropped you releases "The Early Years" tapes, which will surface two years after you become a star, and will no doubt be a collection of unfinished works.

15) ACCOUNTING AND AUDITING RIGHTS

Be sure that your contract requires a periodic accounting from the record company that details your record sales, expenses charged to your account, and royalty payments. Also, insist that the contract allow you to conduct a detailed audit of their numbers. The more rights you have, the better. This can help prevent the record company from becoming sloppy with your account.

16) EXCLUSIVE RECORDING

For contracts with record companies in California, note Civil Code §3423(e) and Code of Civil Procedure §526(5), both of which deal with personal service contracts. Essentially, these code provisions deny a record company the right to obtain an injunction to stop you from recording for another company (even if you agreed to provide the record company with your exclusive services), unless the record company pays you a minimum compensation of $9,000 in the first year, $12,000 in the second year, and substantially more in years three through seven.

9. INDEPENDENT LABEL DEALS WITH MAJOR LABELS

The major label record companies continue to buy most of the worthwhile smaller labels once they reach a certain level. As the cost of recording a viable record comes tumbling down, new independents are constantly cropping up. There are many more labels today that there were just a few years ago. Many of them are nothing more than artists' own "vanity" labels, yet if there is the potential for successful national distribution, a distribution deal may be struck with a major record label.

While there are *many* different types of deals that are entered into between independent labels and major label record companies, they tend to fall into three categories:

INDEPENDENT PRODUCTION AGREEMENTS

An Independent Production Agreement is the agreement an independent label signs with the major label record company to manufacture, distribute, market and promote the record of an artist already signed to the independent label.

The agreement calls for the major label record company to give the independent label a 2% to 5% higher royalty rate than it does on deals done directly with artists, but there is usually a cap on the total payment amount to the independent label. The more services the independent label provides by way of marketing and promoting its artist(s), the higher the royalty rate the independent can negotiate for itself. The independent retains the responsibility to pay the artist(s) their royalties.

If the major label is enamored with the owner of an independent label (e.g., a powerful record producer), or with several of the artists controlled by the independent label, an agreement covering all the artists of the independent label may be entered into.

PROFIT-SPLITTING

Sometimes, rather than entering into an independent production agreement, the independent and major label enter into an arrangement in which the workload and profits are split between them. Under one scenario, the major label may pay for manufacturing and arrange for distribution. It would then charge the independent for all of the costs and retain a percentage of the profit. If the record is ultimately only moderately successful, it is probably economically better for the independent label to have an independent production agreement. If, however, the album is highly successful, it is better for the independent to have a profit-splitting arrangement.

STRAIGHT DISTRIBUTION DEALS

If an independent label wants to gamble, they may enter into a deal with a major label's distribution arm to distribute records for the independent label strictly as a wholesaler. This means that records are sold to the major distributor at a wholesale price, and the distributor marks up the wholesale price before selling it to the record store.

For example, from a typical wholesale price of under $8.00 which the independent label receives (for a CD that retails for $16.98), the independent must pay all of the manufacturing costs, overhead, artist royalties, mechanical royalties to songwriters and publishers, promotion and marketing costs, and any other costs. Whatever is left over is the independent's profit.

BASICS FOR THE SONGWRITER

10. COPYRIGHTS — PROTECTING YOUR SONGS

Remember, the *artist* is paid a royalty from the record company for being the artist on their record. Most often, the artist's royalty rate is a percentage of the suggested retail list price of the record (less a whole bunch of deductions). The person who actually writes a song, whether or not they are an artist, makes money under different arrangements for having written the song.

To understand how money is earned by the songwriter, you must first know a little about copyrights.

YOUR COPYRIGHT MONOPOLY

In the U.S., a copyright is a limited duration monopoly given by the government to the songwriter.[18] As the songwriter, you own a monopoly as it relates to your song. You are Mr. or Ms. "Big," and you call the shots.

---

[18] Technically, the "originator" of the song gets the copyright. The originator may not be the songwriter if the songwriter agreed to write the song as a "work for hire." See the section in this chapter entitled "Works Made For Hire." This comes up most often in connection with film scores and television background music. See Chapters 22 and 23.

To obtain this copyright monopoly, the song (the "work" as it is called by the Copyright Act) has to be "original" and "of sufficient materiality." There are no specific legal tests that define what is original or what is of sufficient materiality. If there is a legal fight about whether a song is "original," a judge or a jury will ultimately determine the issue based in part on their subjective views.

As soon as a "tangible" copy of your song is made, a copyright exists. A tangible copy of a song exists once you have created something you can touch, like a tape or a lead sheet.[19] Technically, you don't have to file anything with the government to obtain a copyright!

Once the copyright exists, the songwriter by law is granted, among other rights, the *exclusive* rights to: (1)reproduce the work (e.g., record the song); (2)distribute copies of the work; and (3)perform the work publicly.[20] This means that no one can do any of the above without the songwriter's permission.[21] By registering a copyrighted song with the U.S. Copyright Office in Washington, D.C., the songwriter[22] can collect compulsory license royalties (discussed in the next subsection), or sue for infringement and collect the fair market value of use and the infringer's profits.[23]

---

[19] A "lead sheet" is a sheet of paper that typically contains the melody, chords and lyrics of a song.

[20] Further rights are listed in §106 of the Copyright Act of 1976.

[21] Congress is holding hearings to determine the best way to protect copyrights in an age of digital transmission since existing copyright laws don't adequately deal with issues surrounding this new technology. Until new laws are enacted, expect to see many lawsuits.

[22] Your publisher may be the one registering the copyright with the Copyright Office if you have transferred copyright ownership to your publisher.

Infringement

It is considered *infringement* for a songwriter to use a portion of someone else's copyrighted song in a new song without permission, unless the new song is legally including only a "fair use" of the copyrighted song, such as on occasion may be the case with a parody. Whether a particular use of a portion of someone else's song constitutes fair use depends on a number of factors, including how much of the copyrighted song is used, in what context it is used, and whether the use of the copyrighted song will deprive the copyright owner of future profits. If you are going to use any part of an older song in your song, obtain permission to do so. Don't rely on the narrow fair use defense.

Obviously, infringement of an existing song defeats copyright protection in the newer song. If it can be shown that the person who claims authorship of a new song had "access"[24] to the older song, (e.g., you heard it on the radio) the remaining legal test is simply whether the amount taken from the older copyrighted song (music or words) was "substantial." This loose standard is applied by the judge or jury when listening to the songs and comparing them.

---

[23] Legal issues surrounding copyright infringement can be complex, with many such issues still being decided by the courts. "Sampling" (i.e., digitally recording a small portion of an existing song), for example, is currently determined by a fairly open-ended standard: if the sound sampled was so distinctive and unusual to be thought of by a judge or a jury as "original," anyone who samples the sound and uses the sample as part of a new song may be guilty of infringement. There are firms, such as EMG Music Clearance and Total Clearance which specialize in obtaining copyright clearances so that you can legally sample someone else's work.

[24] "Access" in the context of infringement is a legal term of art. Access can be shown if a person heard or had knowledge of someone else's work, or had a reasonable opportunity to hear or view the work.

Joint Works

Joint works are those songs that are written by two or more people. If two or more songwriters intend to merge their individual contribution at the time of a song's creation, the writers have created a "joint-work." Each songwriter has the right to license the entire song, subject to paying the other songwriter(s) their share of the royalties, because each owns an undivided interest in the copyright of the entire song.[25]

Even if the writers create separate parts, as when one writes the music and the other writes the lyrics, each is a co-owner of the indivisible whole of the joint work. If, for example, the original lyrics are later completely rejected and a new songwriter writes new lyrics, the original lyricist still owns a part of the new song! This new song is called a "derivative work."[26]

If you want to avoid having someone claim that their contribution to your song was intended to create a joint work, make it clear up front. You do not want any other person claiming an interest in your copyright. For instance, when you are making a demo with the help of a producer or arranger, always clarify that his or her services are being rendered as a producer or arranger, and not as a songwriter.

---

[25] This is discussed in §201(a) of the Copyright Act of 1976.

[26] Technically, a derivative work is a song (or other "work") which is created by the making of modifications or additions to a preexisting work. In the example above, the original lyrics and melody form the preexisting work, while the new songwriter's lyrics together with the original melody comprise the derivative work. If the original lyricist uses the original lyrics with a new melody, it too is a "derivative work."

Arrangements

Arrangements of songs seldom qualify for copyright protection. Under the Copyright Act, arrangements are copyrightable if the arrangement was made by the copyright owner of the song, or the copyright owner of the song consents to allowing the arrangement to be copyrighted. Otherwise, the arrangement itself must be found to be "original" and "of sufficient materiality," not simply an expression of your underlying idea. So, just because your song is recorded in someone else's studio, and they help you produce or arrange your song by adding key instrumental tracks and helping you "phrase" the song just right, that does not mean that they are entitled to a copyrightable interest in either your song or the arrangement of your song.

Works Made For Hire

"Works made for hire," also known as "works for hire," refers to songs written by a songwriter either as an employee or as an independent contractor for someone else. **The person or entity who does the hiring, not the actual songwriter, is the "originator" and "author" of the song, and therefore owns the copyright.** The royalties generated by a song belong to them, not to the actual songwriter, unless the "work for hire" agreement specifically grants the songwriter an interest in royalty income.

---

[27] To meet the requirements of the copyright act, a work for hire contract must be in writing. In other words, you cannot legally enter into a work for hire contract that is not in writing. See §201(b) of the Copyright Act of 1976.

EXCEPTIONS TO YOUR COPYRIGHT MONOPOLY

There are several exceptions under the Copyright Act to a songwriter's "exclusive" monopoly rights. The most important one involves the use of a song on a record.

A license to use the song *must* be granted by the copyright owner if all of the following are true: (1)the song is a "nondramatic" musical composition;[28] (2)the song has been previously recorded and distributed publicly in phonorecords with the copyright owner's permission;[29] and (3)the requested license is for the use of your song in phonorecords only.

The license that must be granted if all of the above is true is referred to as a ***compulsory mechanical license,*** and is the major basis upon which payment by record companies to songwriters and publishers is calculated. If a record company wants to take advantage of a compulsory mechanical license to use your song, it must pay you a royalty in exchange for it.

Note that there is *no* compulsory license for songs used in movies, home videos, on CD-ROMs, DVDs and web sites (internet usage rights are still being worked out). If you do not want your song to be used in a movie, it can't be used.[30] As such,

---

[28] The law does not give the words "dramatic musical composition" clear meaning. You can assume that your song is a "nondramatic musical composition," unless it is written specifically for a musical or an opera. However, even if your song is written for a musical or an opera, it might still be considered a "nondramatic musical composition" if it is later used in a nondramatic fashion (e.g., played on the radio).

[29] Pursuant to the Copyright Act, "phonorecord" means every form of recording (CDs, tapes, etc.) except recordings "accompanying a motion picture or other audiovisual work."

for example, you are free to charge a film company whatever you want (or whatever they are willing to pay).

THE COPYRIGHT NOTICE

Legally, in the U.S., you don't have to put any copyright notice on songs first "published" on or after March 1, 1989.[31] But, giving notice does serve to inform others that the song is yours, and also allows for certain benefits in court should someone infringe on your song. Though not required, I also recommend that you place a copyright notice on your demos. It appears more professional. The symbol for a notice of copyright in a song is ©, and the symbol for a notice of copyright in a sound recording is ℗. Here's how you place a copyright notice:

If you are protecting anything that is "visibly perceptible" (i.e., you can see it), use the symbol ©. You should use this symbol on lead sheets, J-cards, sheet music and albums (if lyrics are printed and to protect the "artwork"). For example, on my lead sheets, I would put: © **2004 David Naggar**

If you are protecting the sound recording itself (which is not visibly perceptible), use the symbol ℗. Put this notice on the surface, label or container of the CD. If your CD, DVD, or even an old cassette has artwork that you wish to protect, add the symbol ©. On my CD I would put: ℗ © **2004 David Naggar**

---

[30] Other compulsory licenses involve cable television, public television (PBS) and jukeboxes. There are also compulsory license requirements for certain digital transmissions of sound recordings (e.g., on internet radio) pursuant to the Digital Performance Right In Sound Recordings Act of 1995, and the Digital Millennium Copyright Act.

[31] "Publication" is defined by the Copyright Act as "the distribution of copies of phonorecords of a work to the public by sale or other transfer of ownership, or by rental, lease, or lending."

For a copyright notice to be effective in the U.S., you must include: (1)the letter C or P inside a circle;[32] (2)the year of "publication" (publication generally occurs when the song is distributed to the public); and (3)the name(s) of the copyright owner(s). All three must be included.

COPYRIGHT REGISTRATION FORMS

Although material can be protected by simply using the © or ℗ symbols, in order to collect compulsory license royalties or sue for infringement, a copyright must also be registered with the Copyright Office. The fee is $30 per registration, but you can register a collection of your songs as one "work" and save a lot of money. To obtain the forms necessary to register a copyright, telephone the Copyright Office at (202) 707-3000, write to: Information and Publication Section LM-455, Copyright Office, Library of Congress, Washington, D.C. 20559, or download the forms from the internet. The web address is www. loc.gov/copyright. The correct form to initially register a song is form PA. If you wish to register both the song *and* the recording you are submitting at the same time, use form SR.

THE DURATION OF A COPYRIGHT

A copyright for works created after January 1, 1978 is valid in the U.S. for the life of the last surviving author plus 70 years.

Copyright protection for works first published and registered with the Copyright Office between January 1, 1964

---

[32] You can also use the word copyright or copr. instead of the letter C inside a circle.

and December 31, 1977 is valid initially for 28 years. There is an automatic renewal of the copyright protection for an additional 67 years at the expiration of the 28 year period.[33] Thus, the total copyright protection is 95 years from the date of publication.

U.S. copyright protection for all works published before January 1, 1964 has either expired (which means that the works are in the public domain and anyone can use them for free),[34] or has already been properly extended with the Copyright Office (which means that the copyright is valid for 95 years from the date of publication).[35] Anyone can freely use any song in the U.S. which was registered by an American author before 1923,[36] and any work registered by an American author between 1923 and 1963 for which a proper application to extend copyright protection was not filed with the Copyright Office.

Now that you know how to protect your songs, let's discuss sending out your demo CDs.

---

[33] Because of burden of proof issues that arise in a court of law, and because of issues relating to derivative works, it is better practice to actually file a renewal notice.

[34] Once a song is in the public domain, the copyright owner is no longer entitled to any royalty payment.

[35] The duration of a copyright on works for hire is the lesser of 95 years from publication or 120 years from creation.

[36] The Sony Bono Copyright Extension Act, which became law in 1998, extended the life of a copyright in the U.S. by 20 years for songs registered in 1923 and thereafter. In other words, the copyright used to last for the life of the author plus 50 years. Older works had 75 years, not 95 years of protection. Songs registered by American authors in 1922 and before did not benefit from this extra 20 years of protection and have fallen into the public domain, at least for use in the U.S. Because of an international agreement entered into in 1994 (the General Agreement on Tariffs and Trade (GATT)), foreign works first published abroad before 1923 may in certain situations retain copyright protection in the U.S. for 95 year from when first registered.

11. SENDING OUT YOUR SONGS

As a songwriter, your goal is to get your songs on a record.

If you do not have an active publisher, material you send directly to anybody who can actually help you earn money from your song (including a publisher) will generally not be listened to no matter how good it is, unless it is first solicited. People in the business are afraid to be the target of a frivolous lawsuit by someone who later claims that their song was stolen.

Initially, it is best to have someone in the business end of the music industry, such as a music attorney, send out your material because it lends more credibility to your songs. A great song can, however, occasionally speak for itself, even if it does come directly from you.

If you do send out your own CDs, you should try to send them to those who are as close to the decision-making source as possible! If an artist is established, the artist, their personal manager, or the producer of the artist's last album, is *much* more likely than a publisher or an A & R representative to ultimately decide what goes on the artist's record.

If, on the other hand, an artist is unknown and newly signed, the record company is likely to dictate which songs ultimately appear on the artist's record. Remember though, if you haven't received permission to send your demo, it probably won't be listened to by anybody. Here are two of the better sources to help a songwriter send a demo to the right place. Unfortunately, to get your hands on either of them will cost over $100:

Pollstar

POLLSTAR, 4697 W. Jacquelyn Ave., Fresno, CA 93722; tel. (559) 271-7900; web address: www.pollstar.com. POLLSTAR concentrates on providing concert tour information, but subscribers also receive "Contact Directories," which include record company rosters, music radio directories and agency directories. The Contact Directory that is most valuable is the one directory not included in the cost of the subscription, but rather, requires the payment of an additional fee. POLLSTAR calls it the "Confidential Artist Management Roster." The Roster gives current phone numbers, fax numbers and addresses of artists' managers.

Billboard International Talent And Touring Directory

Billboard Directories, P.O. Box 2011, Marion, OH 43306; tel. (800) 745-8922; web address www.billboard.com. This guide, published annually, lists hundreds of artists, together with booking agents, personal managers and record companies. There is also a section on where to contact the agents and managers.

PUBLISHER AND A & R NAMES

The Music Registry is a *great* source of industry names (but not for artist and artist management contact information). There are actually four registries which list names, addresses and phone numbers of music business players: one for A & R, one for publishers, one for legal and business affairs, and one for film and television music. The Music Business Registry, Inc., 7510 Sunset Blvd., Suite 1041, Los Angeles CA 90046; tel. (800) 377-7411; web address www.musicregistry.com.

♪ ♪ ♪

Also, important tidbits can often be found in the major industry trade magazine, *Billboard*. Other good sources of information are *The Musician's Atlas*, which lists many industry contacts, *Radio and Records* and *Hits Magazine*. (For example, every year, the August issue of *Hits Magazine* lists the phone numbers of many artists' managers with cross-references to the artists.)

12. PRIMARY SOURCES OF INCOME

A songwriter makes money by selling, generally through his or her publisher, rights to use one or more of the songwriter's songs. In most circumstances, in order to get paid, a publishing entity which owns the legal copyright to the song must be specified. A songwriter may act as his or her own publisher. (See Chapter 16, "Creating Your Own Publishing Company.") Often, however, the songwriter can generate substantially more income from a song by associating with a major publishing company.

Profits generated from a song are split between the songwriter and the publisher (even if you act as your own publisher). Through quirks of history, the holder(s) of the *publisher's share* (regardless of who owns the "publishing" — i.e., the copyright rights) are generally said to receive 50% of the song's profits. The remaining 50% is said to be the *writer's share*. Notwithstanding the use of the terms *publisher's share* and *writer's share*, the actual profits split between a songwriter and a "real" publisher vary greatly depending on the arrangement between them. Very often, the songwriter receives a large portion of the *publisher's share*. Therefore, in this chapter I will discuss the total money generated by a song. I will discuss the role of publishers in more detail in Chapter 14.

The two primary sources of income for songs are: (1) *"mechanical"* royalties paid by the record company for using the songwriter's song on one of its records; and (2) *"performing"* royalties paid by television stations, radio stations, night clubs, restaurants, internet web broadcasters, and others for playing the songwriter's song publicly. Note that "performing" royalties are not paid by artists for performing a song, though technically, an artist could be held accountable to make such a payment.

1) MECHANICAL ROYALTIES

In exchange for mechanical rights (i.e., the rights to reproduce a song in records), record companies pay mechanical royalties to the copyright owner of a song. The copyright owner is the songwriter or any person or entity to whom the songwriter assigns the legal copyright ownership.

The amount of the payment is typically negotiated between the record company and the copyright owner. However, if the criteria discussed in the "Exceptions To Your Copyright Monopoly" section of Chapter 10 are met, a copyright owner *must* license his or her song to any record company that agrees to pay the compulsory mechanical license rate set by statute. Currently, the rate per song is the larger of (1)8.5¢, or (2)1.65¢ per minute of playing time (or fraction thereof) for each record sold.[37]

For example, if your 3-minute song was licensed to a record company under the terms of a *compulsory* mechanical license for use on an album that sold 100,000 copies, a record company would be obligated to pay the copyright owner $8,500 (100,000 x 8.5¢) in mechanical royalties.

---

[37] The rates are scheduled to increase on January 1, 2006, to the larger of (1)9.1¢, or 1.75¢ per minute.

If your 6-1/2-minute song was licensed to a record company under the terms of a compulsory mechanical license for use on an album that sold 2,000,000 copies, a record company would be obligated to pay the copyright owner $231,000 (2,000,000 x 1.65¢ x 7) in mechanical royalties.

If you co-wrote four 3-minute songs with a friend, and each of the songs was licensed to a record company under the terms of a compulsory mechanical license for use on an album that sold 500,000 copies (a gold album), a record company would be obligated to pay the copyright owners $170,000 (500,000 x 4 songs x 8.5¢) in mechanical royalties. You and your publisher (the owners of an undivided 1/2 interest in the copyright) would receive $85,000 (half of the $170,000). Your friend (and his or her publisher) would receive the other half.[38]

Of course, record companies do not want to pay the full statutory amount, and so they attempt to negotiate agreements with copyright owners that call for payment of a reduced rate. If they do not agree to pay the full statutory amount, however, the copyright owner can refuse to allow the record company to use the song.

The predominant way in which a record company forces a reduction in the amount of mechanical royalties it has to pay a songwriter is contained in the so-called *controlled composition*

---

[38] Compulsory mechanical licenses are hardly ever used! It is easier for a copyright owner to monitor direct licenses. It is also easier for record companies to deal with direct licenses because the compulsory accounting rules are considered too time-consuming. The statutory compulsory mechanical license rate is important because it sets the standard for the mechanical rates that record companies actually do pay.

clause of a record contract between the artist and the record company.

A *controlled composition* is a song written, owned or controlled, in whole or in part, by the artist. Since, unlike artist royalties, the record company cannot "recoup" anything from a *songwriter's* mechanical royalties,[39] record companies typically insist that the artist (with the exception of major stars) agree to license songs that are controlled by the artist for 75% of the minimum statutory rate. In other words, no matter how long the song is, the record company will pay only 6.375¢ (75% x 8.5¢). Often, they pay only 4.25¢ (50% x 8.5¢) for mid-line and budget records. Also, the controlled composition clause will often limit the record company's total mechanical royalty payments on any album to one of the following: (1)the number of songs actually on the album x 6.375¢ (75% of the statutory rate), (2)76.5¢ (12 x 6.375¢) or (3)63.75¢ (10 x 6.375¢), depending on the artist's negotiating strength.[40]

If an artist uses songs from an outside songwriter (i.e., a non-controlled composition) and the outside songwriter insists on getting the full statutory amount (8.5¢), then the artist is very likely to end up receiving less than 75% of 8.5¢ on the songs the artist *has* written. The artist will receive, as income earned in his or her capacity as a songwriter, only what is left over from the mechanical royalty "pie" allotted for all of the songs written for the entire album. If a typical controlled

---

[39] Money isn't "advanced" by the record company to the songwriter in the same way it is advanced to the artist.

[40] Also, the record company will insist that no mechanical royalties on controlled compositions be paid on "free goods."

composition clause is included as part of the record contract, mechanical royalties paid by the record company in excess of 76.5¢ or 63.75¢ per album, depending on the deal, may be charged as an advance against the artist's other royalties. This is complicated but important to know, because if an artist puts a song from an outside songwriter on the album, it can hurt the artist financially. And, if the artist does not think putting the outside songwriter's song on the album will make the artist more money than if the song was not on the album, the song won't be there.

Here's an example: Suppose an artist's deal with the record company states that mechanical royalties paid in excess of 63.75¢ per album will be charged as an advance against the artist's other royalties. Also, for purposes of this example, assume that there are 12 songs on the album — 6 written by the artist, and 6 written by an outside songwriter who insists on receiving the full statutory mechanical royalty rate of 8.5¢.

Six outside songwriter songs (8.5¢ x 6)	51.00¢
Six songs written by artist (75% x 8.5¢ x 6)	+38.25¢
Total mechanical royalties payable by record company per album	89.25¢
Less: Per album mechanical pie (as agreed to in the artist's record contract)	− 63.75¢
Amount payable in excess of album mechanical pie (charged as an advance against artist's other royalties)	= 25.50¢
Net amount per album artist will actually receive for writing six songs on the album (38.25¢ minus 25.5¢)	12.75¢

As you can see, the business reality of the controlled

composition clause often forces all but the most sought after outside songwriters to accept a reduced mechanical royalty rate equal to 6.375¢ per song. Even sought after songwriters often accept a reduced mechanical royalty rate of 6.375¢ for sales of mid-line or budget records.[41]

2) PERFORMING ROYALTIES

In exchange for the right to play songs in public, television stations, radio stations, night clubs and other public users of music, such as companies broadcasting on the internet and companies that provide elevator music, pay performing royalties.

Until recently *every* nightclub, restaurant and other place you heard music publicly was charged a fee.[42] Since it would be too cumbersome for every public user of music to enter into a separate royalty agreement with each copyright owner of music, *performance rights societies* that represent the interests of songwriters and their publishers have come into existence.[43]

Songwriters and their publishers affiliate independently with a performance rights society.[44] In the U.S., ASCAP and

[41] Canada has its own rates, but are generally economically tied to the U.S. rates. Except for the U.S. and Canada, most countries have entirely different copyright royalty systems. "Mechanicals" in these other countries are a set percentage of the retail price of the record.

[42] As part of the Sony Bono Copyright Term Extension Act, under certain circumstances, restaurants and bars of less than 3,750 sq. ft. and retail stores of less than 2,000 sq. ft. don't have to pay a fee. However, the World Trade Organization has ruled that this law violates U.S. international copyright obligations to the European Union (EU). For now, the U.S. is compensating the EU for this violation, but ultimately the EU is pushing the U.S. to change its law.

[43] For political reasons, performance rights societies do not collect royalties for music performed in films playing in U.S. theaters.

BMI are the dominant performance rights societies.[45] Both are non-profit organizations. Other countries have their equivalent societies.

For each public user of music, each society negotiates a separate licensing agreement. Most of the licensing agreements allow the public user to use all of the songs of all the copyright owners the society represents for a negotiated set fee.

The society collects the "performing" royalties from each public user, deducts the society's expenses (about 20% of the money collected), and distributes the remainder to its songwriter and publisher members. Of the amount distributed, the songwriter members receive 50% and the publisher members receive 50%. Unlike the record companies who pay mechanical royalties to a publisher, who in turn pays the songwriter his or her agreed share, the performance rights societies pay affiliated songwriter members 50% directly (in addition to paying the publisher members 50% directly). As an individual songwriter, depending on your deal with your publisher, you may be entitled to part of your publisher's share of performing royalties, but these royalties will need to be collected from the publisher directly, not from the performance rights society.

---

[44] As a songwriter, you can be affiliated with only one society at any given time, and, generally, your application will not be accepted by a society unless you have a song on a record that is, or will soon be, sold publicly. If a songwriter acts as his or her own publisher, a separate affiliation in their capacity as publisher is required.

[45] SESAC is the other performance rights society in the United States. It, however, controls a tiny percentage of U.S. performing rights. For clarity, I have limited my discussion to ASCAP and BMI, but the information given also applies to SESAC (with the exception that SESAC is actually a for-profit organization).

Allocation Of Royalty License Proceeds Among The Society's Members

For most performances of music, ASCAP and BMI pay songwriter members, and publisher members, quarterly (i.e., four times a year). Payment occurs within six to nine months after the end of the three month period in which the performing monies were earned. Generally, even though most public users of music are charged a license fee, both ASCAP and BMI calculate payment to their members for performances in clubs, bars and restaurants based on complicated formulas that rely solely on a song's radio and television airplay. Also, these societies use very different methods of calculating which songs, and which songwriter members, are entitled to what percentage of the income that will ultimately be distributed to the various songwriters.[46] Because each songwriter's situation is unique, it is difficult to say which society pays its songwriters more in any given year. Once it becomes generally known that one society is paying a bit more than the other, the payments tend to equalize. Therefore, which society will ultimately be more beneficial to a new songwriter cannot be said with any degree of certainty.

To give you a rough idea of the dollars involved, a fairly popular BMI song played on commercial radio generates at least 6¢ per play. If the station's BMI license fee is in the top 25% of license fees paid to BMI by commercial radio stations, then the song will generate no less that 12¢ of income per play. ASCAP's formulas defy calculation in this simple manner, but payments seem to equalize anyway.

---

[46] Descriptions of the various factors and formulas that determine the actual payment to songwriters can be found at the ASCAP and BMI web sites: www.ascap.com and www.bmi.com, respectively.

If a song reaches number 1 on *Billboard's* "Hot 100," it is likely to be played publicly enough times in the first year of release to generate $250,000 to $500,000 in performing royalties (50% of this amount will be paid directly to the songwriter member(s) who wrote the song, and 50% will be paid to the publisher member(s) who published the song).

If a song only reaches number 20, it is likely to be played publicly enough times to generate $60,000 to $120,000 in performing royalties. If it tops out at number 100, it is likely to be played publicly only enough times to generate $5,000 to $10,000 in performing royalties.

As mentioned earlier a songwriter may be entitled to part of his or her publisher's share of performing royalties, but these royalties will need to be collected from the publisher directly, not from the performance rights society.

13. SECONDARY SOURCES OF INCOME

FOREIGN MECHANICAL RIGHTS

Foreign royalties are becoming a larger percentage of the songwriter's profit picture as sales of U.S. artists' records boom internationally.

Most countries have mechanical rights collection organizations that license all musical compositions. Unlike the U.S., where mechanical licenses are based on a statutory rate per song, the mechanical amount collected in most foreign countries is based on a percentage of the retail price of a record. Foreign publishers are generally used to collect royalty monies earned in other countries because they are more aware of the nuances particular to a local country. Foreign publishers acting in this capacity are referred to as "sub-publishers" because they are accountable in the performance of their duties to the U.S. publisher.

FOREIGN PERFORMING RIGHTS

Most every country has its own equivalent of ASCAP and BMI. ASCAP and BMI enter into contracts with these societies to collect monies for ASCAP and BMI *songwriters*. A little over 25% of all performing monies received by ASCAP and BMI come from foreign societies, and this percentage is increasing rapidly.

Generally, large *publishers* contract with foreign sub-publishers to collect the publisher's share of foreign performing royalties from each country's performing rights society because payment is much quicker than if the publisher contracted with the foreign performing rights societies directly. In a typical sub-publisher deal, the sub-publisher keeps 15% to 25% of the monies earned.

SYNCHRONIZATION LICENSE FEES

In exchange for a fee, a *synchronization ("sync") license* is issued to companies, such as those producing television shows, movies, advertisements, CD-ROMs, DVDs, web sites and home videos, that wish to synchronize a songwriter's music to their visual images. But remember, a songwriter does not have to license the use of his or her songs to these users. There is no compulsory requirement to do so. That is why these fees are very fluid and depend on who needs who.

As an example, for national television commercials, a well-known song can earn from $50,000 to well over $1,000,000 for use in a major advertisement campaign. The same song will earn $20,000 to $70,000 if used as the theme song of a major film; $10,000 to $50,000 if used somewhere in a film but not as the theme song; and typically less than $1,800 if used on television.

The sync fees for television are lower than those for film because (1)television budgets are lower, (2)television reaches a much wider audience and therefore reaches more potential record buyers, and (3)a song used on television will generate extra performing royalties.

The sync fees for CD-ROMs, DVDs and web sites are all over the board, as I will discuss in Chapters 24 and 25.

SHEET MUSIC

The royalty paid by a sheet music company is typically 20% of the retail selling price for sheet music containing a single song. Today, this equals 79¢ (20% of $3.95 — the typical retail price of sheet music).[47]

Folios are collections of songs. The total royalty paid by sheet music companies for the songs included in a folio ranges from 10% to 12-1/2% of the retail selling price of the folio. Folios can be "mixed," "matching" or "personality" folios. A "mixed folio" is a collection of well-known songs made popular by various artists. A "matching folio" is a collection of songs from a particular album. "Personality folios" are those that have the artist's picture on the cover. In personality folios, a 15% royalty is typically paid to the artist (for the use of the songs as well as the artist's name and likeness). *Instructional print music* (e.g., "How to play the piano" folios) bears a 10% royalty payment.[48]

---

[47] As we enter the era of the global economy, more and more major publishing companies are able to receive 20% of the retail selling price on sheet music sold outside of the U.S. and Canada as well.

[48] There are four major manufactures of secular printed music in the U.S.: Cherry Lane Music, Hal Leonard Corp., Music Sales Corp., and Warner Brothers.

14. MUSIC PUBLISHING

PUBLISHERS

If you are like most artists and songwriters, you probably wonder what exactly publishers do and why so many people who have never made money in the music business tell you to "hang on to your publishing."

There is a lot more to publishing than filling out ASCAP/BMI forms and copyright registration forms. Full-service publishing companies find artists, record companies, film companies, television production companies, advertisers, producers of CD-ROMs and DVDs, internet users, and others to use a songwriter's song. They negotiate licenses with anyone using the song and ensure that proper royalties are paid. They also monitor the song's public usage to make sure it is properly reported to the performance rights society, so that performing royalties are not lost. In short, a good full-service publisher generates more income from a song than the songwriter could, and also, the songwriter's time is freed up to write new songs.

Typically, in exchange for doing all of the above for the songwriter, a publisher insists that the songwriter transfer all of his or her official copyright "rights" (i.e., the rights of the copyright owner) to the publisher. The publisher and the songwriter then split the profits generated by the song. Review the "Your Copyright Monopoly" section of Chapter 10 for a refresher on the rights transferred.

Historically, the publisher received 50% of the song's profits. Over time, as the record industry has matured, the role of publishers is not as important as it once was. Many artists now write their own songs and act as their own publishers. Other well-known songwriters do not need someone to find a recording artist for them; to the contrary, the artists seek them out. So today, for successful songwriters with an established track record, major publishing companies are, in essence, little more than financing companies, advancing the songwriters money in exchange for anticipated profits from a song. The songwriter receives a steady income, and the publisher and songwriter agree to split the publishing share of income.

If, for example, the songwriter and publishing company agree to "split the publishing" 50/50, then the songwriter retains 75% of the profits earned from the song (100% of the songwriter's share of profits, and 50% of the publisher's share of profits).

Nevertheless, as I mentioned earlier, through quirks of history, the holder(s) of the *publisher's share* (regardless of who owns the "publishing" — i.e., the copyright rights) are generally said to receive 50% of the song's profits. The remaining 50% is said to be the *writer's share*. This is why the songwriter receives 50% of the performing royalties (i.e., the writer's share) directly from ASCAP or BMI. Even if the songwriter has a contract with a publishing company that states that the songwriter is retaining an interest in the publisher's share, the full publisher's share of performing royalties is generally paid by ASCAP or BMI directly to the major publishing company.[49] It is up to the songwriter to make sure that the publishing company pays the songwriter his or her portion of the retained publisher's share.

---

[49] ASCAP and BMI will not typically make payments directly to a publishing company which is created by the writer in order to share the "publishing" with a major publishing company.

A major publishing company has many departments to ensure that the publisher's entire operation runs smoothly. The publisher's paperwork (e.g., registering songs with the copyright office, issuing licenses, making sure that the correct amount of royalties are being paid for the songs and disbursed to the writers) is handled by a combination of departments including what are often called the Business/Legal Affairs Department, the Copyright Department and the Royalties Department. Placing the publisher's songs with users, finding new songwriters, and improving the songwriter's songs so that the publisher has new songs to sell, are all handled by what is typically called the Creative Department.

EMI and Warner/Chappell are the biggest music publishers. These two companies own the rights to, and have to keep track of, literally tens of thousands of songs. Every time you hear the song "Happy Birthday" in a movie or on television, Warner/Chappell makes money. (Wouldn't you love to own the rights to that song?)

Universal Music (MCA), BMG and Sony are also industry heavyweights, however, because becoming a publishing company is not as financially difficult as becoming a record company, the publishing industry is not dominated by publishing companies the way the record industry is dominated by the "majors."

Essentially, there are only two key parts to a publishing company:

Administrative — to take care of the paperwork.
Creative — to find the writers, improve their songs and to run around schmoozing people in order to get songs recorded or used in movies and television.

That is why a publishing company does not have to be big to be successful. A song on a record label that lacks sufficient market presence and financial backing will not be widely heard, no matter how great the song is. A publishing company does not require the financial backing that a record company does. A publisher need only enter into a mechanical licensing agreement with a record company to place a song on an album. The marketing and promotion of the album will be financially supported by the record company.

You may have heard of the Harry Fox Agency. The Harry Fox Agency is a part of the National Music Publishers Association, which issues mechanical licenses for most publishers in the U.S., ensures that mechanical royalties are paid, and accounts to the publishers. They also perform occasional audits of the record companies to make sure that the right amount of mechanical royalties are being paid. For its services, as of April 1, 2004, the Harry Fox Agency charges 6.75% of the royalties distributed. It has particularly useful information about issuing mechanical licenses in the FAQ (frequently asked questions) link at its web site: www.harryfox.com

SONGWRITER DEALS WITH PUBLISHERS

When you are entering into a contract to give up part of your publishing, make sure that the publisher is providing you with a service that you anticipate will generate more money to you than you would otherwise receive if you did not do the deal. If you do not believe that a particular publisher will make you money, do not enter into the contract!

There may be any number of reasons to have someone else handle your publishing. You may not want to do your own administrative paperwork. (It's a pain to do.) You may not have the contacts to get your song(s) to artists and other users of music, or, you may not be able to get an independent label to take you on as an artist, unless you offset some of their risk by including some of your publishing. All of these reasons are valid. The important thing is to know why you are entering into the deal and to make sure that whoever you deal with makes you more money than you would otherwise make.[50]

A deal may be for a single song, where a songwriter and publisher agree to enter into a deal covering only one of the songwriter's songs. Another type of deal binds the songwriter as an *exclusive* songwriter for the publishing company for a specific period of time. This means that the publishing company will be the publisher of every song the songwriter writes during the

---

50 Along the same lines, do not be surprised if an artist who "picks up" your song changes a few of the words and asks to be included as a songwriter on the song. Remember, it is about money. If you need the artist more than the artist needs your song, it may be worth including the artist as one of the songwriters of the song. A co-writer of one song on a Madonna album makes much more than a writer of many songs that appear on an album of a lesser-known artist.

term of their agreement. A variation of the exclusive songwriter deal is a writer-artist development deal, where the publisher is actively trying to land a record deal for the songwriter who is also an artist. If the publisher is successful in getting a record deal for the songwriter/artist, presumably many of the songwriter/publisher-owned songs will be on the album.

Often, songwriters receive advances from a full-service publishing company on the anticipated income stream their songs are expected to generate. If the songwriter is an exclusive songwriter for the publishing company, this provides the songwriter with a steady income that frees the songwriter from monthly economic worry. As part of this type of deal with a full-service publishing company, a new songwriter may be expected to give up all of his or her interest in the publisher's share (i.e., 50% of the gross dollars earned). This, however, may not be necessary if the publisher believes in your songs and you are willing to take smaller advances against anticipated income from royalties. Advances for new aspiring songwriters, who are not also *artists*, rarely exceed $2,000 per month, and for the most part, are paid only in Nashville. Outside of Nashville, unless the songwriter is already a signed recording artist (or an aspiring artist for whom the major publishing company believes it can land a record deal), or the songwriter has a unique "in" with a major recording artist, a major publishing company is not likely to offer the songwriter any deal.

There are many nuances that define the various deals a songwriter may enter into with a publisher. Songwriters often enter into what are referred to as *co-publishing* deals and *administrative* deals. These terms mean different things to different people in the industry, and what they mean must be spelled out in each contract.

A *co-publishing* deal is entered into by a songwriter and a publisher when the songwriter and publisher agree to share the publishing. This type of deal is often entered into when the songwriter's songs are expected to generate a lot of income for the publishing company, and the songwriter has his or her own outlets for the songs. Typically, in deals such as this, the publisher's share of income is split 50/50. This means that the songwriter retains 75% of the songs' earning power (i.e., 100% of the songwriter's share and 50% of the publisher's share).

If a straight *administration* deal is entered into by a songwriter and a publisher, there will be no advances, and the publishing company will limit its role to administrative tasks. Copyright ownership of the songs may be retained by a separate publishing entity controlled by the songwriter, the term of the agreement may be shorter, and a lesser percentage of publishing (i.e., the publisher's share) will be given to the administrative publishing company. Typically, the administrative publisher receives 7-1/2% to 20% of the gross dollars earned in such deals. The more income a songwriter's songs have generated in previous years, the lower the publisher's percentage. Also, the specific services rendered play a part in determining the percentage earned by the publishing company. For instance, Bug International, a publishing company that specializes in administrative deals and typically charges 10% to 15%, does help songwriters find users for their songs, a function considered "creative."

15. KEY PUBLISHING CONTRACT DEAL POINTS

As with the key record contract deal points, the key points discussed below, to one extent or another, deal with whether money ends up in the songwriter's pocket or in the publisher's pocket. (Remember, a songwriter may own part of his or her own publishing too.)

Keep this list as a handy reference tool when you are negotiating, or renegotiating, your publishing deal. Insist that your lawyer explain each item to you in detail.

1) TERM

The term of an exclusive songwriter deal with a major publisher will usually be for one year, and gives the publisher the right to exercise several consecutive one-year options. Try to limit the number of options to three or fewer. A writer-artist development deal may be for as long as two years. This allows the publisher more time to get the songwriter a record deal. If it is successful, the publishing house will generally insist on having an option to extend the publishing agreement for the life of the record deal.

2) RIGHTS TRANSFERRED / USE OF SONG(S)

The publisher will want all of the songwriter's rights transferred to it. There are some rights that you may not wish your publisher to exercise. You may wish to limit your publisher's right to do one or more of the following without your approval:

a.   Change the title of the song.
b.   Change the words or music.
c.   Allow it to be synchronized to X-rated films.
d.   Allow it to be synchronized to advertisements.
e.   Translate the words into a foreign language.
f.   Allow someone else to modify your song and share in the royalties from the derivative work.

Also, remember that *compulsory* mechanical licenses to others need not be issued until the song has first been recorded and distributed publicly in phonorecords with the copyright owner's permission. A songwriter who is also an artist may want to deny the publisher the right to issue a negotiated license to anyone other than the songwriter until after the songwriter's song has appeared on his or her own album.

Finally, the publisher may ask the songwriter to transfer all rights to all of the songwriter's material written prior to the date the agreement was entered into. If this is the case, make sure that you are being compensated for these additional songs.

3) ROYALTIES

Major publishing companies are often owned by a parent company that owns a major record and/or film company. Make sure that the publisher cannot issue mechanical licenses at less than customary rates to its affiliated companies. Do this even if you are entitled to receive part of the "publisher's share."

Your contract with the publisher should call for "the songwriter" to receive 50% of *all* monies collected (except performing rights monies paid directly to the songwriter from ASCAP or BMI).

4) ADVANCES

If a songwriter signs an agreement with a major publishing company allowing his or her songs to be published by the publishing company, the publishing company may agree to pay the songwriter advances on its anticipated profits from the songwriter's songs. The bigger the percentage of profits given up by the songwriter, the higher the advance should be. The amount of the advance is based on how much money the publishing company expects to make from the songs. The range is from $0 to a high percentage of the money earned by the songwriter's songs in the previous year(s). When a new *artist*, who happens to also be a songwriter, is signed by a major label record company, publishing companies will offer him or her an advance in exchange for a portion of his or her publishing. This amount can be well over $100,000 if the publisher believes that the record company will strongly push the artist/songwriter's record, or if a bidding war breaks out. Of course, the advances will be recoupable from royalties when actually received by the publishing company from licensees.

Often, the publisher negotiates to receive advances from third parties to whom they license the songs. For instance, a record company may give the publishing company an advance against anticipated mechanical royalties that the publishing company and songwriter will earn from a record that is going to be released. The agreement between the songwriter and publisher should include a provision entitling the songwriter to participate in all advances paid to the publisher by third parties for licenses.

5) RESERVE LIMITATIONS

Usually, publishers are paid by record companies quarterly,

and "reserves" of 30% to 40% are retained by the record company. These reserves are often held for as long as two years. Since record companies do not have cross-collateralization rights against publishers, the way they do against artists, most record companies are extremely wary when it comes time to release the reserve to the publishing house. In any event, just because you have a song on a major album, don't expect to see any money immediately.

Even though record companies pay the publisher quarterly, publishers typically try to pay the songwriter only twice a year. Every effort should be made to get your publisher to pay you quarterly.

6) COPYRIGHT OWNERSHIP REVERSION

Generally, the rights to your song(s) are sold to the publisher for the life of the copyright in exchange for your participation in royalty payments.[51] You should try to negotiate for reversion of the copyright if certain criteria are not met by the publisher (e.g., placing a song on a record within a certain time period).

7) WORK FOR HIRE

Remember, the copyright of a "work for hire" is owned from the outset by the person or entity doing the hiring, not the

---

[51] If the original owner of a copyrighted work created after January 1, 1978 sends timely notice to the publisher, the publishing rights revert back to the original owner after 35 years. (The notice can be sent as early as 10 years before the effective date of the reversion.) The additional 39 years for older copyrighted works also revert back to the original copyright owner upon giving effective notice.

actual songwriter. Make sure that your publishing contract specifically states that your songs are not works for hire and are not written within the scope of employment by the publisher. Even if a publisher offers to pay you your share of royalties in exchange for making your songs works for hire, it is not in your best interest to do so. If one of your songs becomes a standard, it will have value for many years. One of the quirks in the copyright law allows the original owner of a song to reclaim full copyright ownership after 35 years.[52] If you are not the original owner, you will not be entitled to exercise this right of copyright reversion.[53]

8) MINIMUM SONG DELIVERY

In most publishing contracts, especially those in which a publishing company is paying the songwriter an advance, a minimum song delivery requirement is added to ensure that the songwriter is actually working. Typically, this averages about twelve songs per year (one per month). In a situation where you write a song with someone else (i.e., collaborations), you will only receive credit for having written half of a song.

9) COLLABORATIONS

Make sure that there are no prohibitions against collaborating with songwriters who have other publishers. You should only be responsible for transferring your share of ownership of the collaborated song to the publisher.

---

[52] See footnote 51.

[53] Never allow your song to be referred to in any contract as a "work for hire," unless you are being paid considerable money for a particular project (e.g., to work on a film).

10) EXCEPTIONS TO EXCLUSIVITY

Even though a songwriter's agreement may be exclusive, there may be certain situations that you wish to exclude from your agreement with the publisher. For instance, if you are writing a song specifically for a film, oftentimes the film company will insist on receiving the copyright and you may need this flexibility.

Also, for contracts with publishers in California, be aware of Civil Code §3423(e) and Code of Civil Procedure §526(5), both of which deal with personal service contracts. Essentially, these code provisions deny a publisher the right to obtain an injunction to stop you from writing for someone else (even if you agreed to provide the publisher your exclusive services), unless the publisher pays you a minimum compensation of $9,000 in the first year, $12,000 in the second year, and substantially more in years three through seven.

11) CO-PUBLISHING ISSUES

A co-publishing deal is entered into not only when a songwriter keeps part of his or her publishing, but also if two "real" publishing companies are publishers of a song (e.g., when each songwriter that collaborates on a song has a different publisher).

If there is a co-publishing deal, two major issues arise apart from "official" ownership of the copyright. The first issue is who is entitled to "administer" the song (and gets paid to do so). It is always better to have you, or your publisher, keep the administration.

The other major issue is determining what monies get divided among the various publishers. This amount can be disputed because each publisher may be performing different functions and incurring different costs in doing so.

12) INFRINGEMENT CLAIMS

We live in a lawsuit-happy society. Anyone can claim that you infringed on their song and start a costly legal battle. A publishing company will generally insist on (1)being indemnified by you for the full costs of the lawsuit, (2)retaining control over the litigation, and (3)holding as a "reserve" (instead of paying you) the money that is being sued for, regardless of whether the lawsuit is justified or not. At the very least, a songwriter should insist that if the lawsuit is unsuccessful, the publisher will pay for its share of the legal fees.

13) LIMITS ON FOREIGN SUB-PUBLISHER FEES

Most publishers use foreign sub-publishers to collect royalties from other countries because of the nuances particular to each country. If the agreement between the songwriter and publisher states that the songwriter and publisher are to split the net foreign royalties received by the publisher (after the sub-publisher takes its fees), then the songwriter, at least to some extent, is really paying for publishing twice. A songwriter should try to receive royalties *"at the source."* This means that the songwriter will share royalties 50/50 *before* the sub-publisher's share is deducted.

14) ACCOUNTING AND AUDITING RIGHTS

You should be sure your contract requires a periodic accounting from the publishing company that details (1)payments received from record companies, (2)other licensing fees received by the publisher for use of your songs, (3)payments from sub-publishers, and (4)expenses charged to your account. Also, insist that the contract allow you to conduct a detailed audit of the publisher's books. The more rights you have, the better. This can help prevent the publishing company from becoming sloppy with your account.

16. CREATING YOUR OWN PUBLISHING COMPANY

Here is a basic guide to creating your own publishing company. There are three essential steps:

1. If you are a songwriter and are setting up your own publishing company, before you do anything else, first apply for affiliation with a performance rights society. The reason to do this is because if the name of your company is similar to others, ASCAP/BMI will turn the application down (i.e., they will not collect money for you). It is therefore smart to apply before your company has spent money on promotional material.

You must apply *separately* as a songwriter and as a publisher to the *same* performance rights society (i.e., apply to either ASCAP as both a songwriter and publisher *or* apply to BMI as both a songwriter and publisher). If your intention is to become a publishing company for other songwriters as well, separate applications as a publisher to both ASCAP and BMI should be made, and two different publishing company names must be chosen and used. It can take over a month to get approved.

ASCAP and BMI will provide you with lists of names currently being used by publishing companies affiliated with them. BMI will even reserve a company name for you (upon request and for a limited time only) if it is not being used by another publisher.

You can contact ASCAP and BMI as follows:

ASCAP:

One Lincoln Plaza, New York, NY 10023;
tel. (212) 621-6000; fax (212) 724-9064; or

7920 Sunset Blvd, 3rd Floor, Los Angeles, CA 90046;
tel. (323) 883-1000; fax (323) 883-1049; or

Two Music Square West, Nashville, TN 37203;
tel. (615) 742-5000; fax (615) 742-5020.

ASCAP's internet address is: www.ascap.com
also, tel. (800) 95ASCAP

BMI:

320 West 57th Street, New York, NY 10019;
tel. (212) 586-2000; fax (212) 245-8986; or

8730 Sunset Blvd, 3rd Floor, West Hollywood, CA
90069;
tel. (310) 659-9109; fax (310) 657-6947; or

10 Music Square East, Nashville, TN 37203;
tel. (615) 401-2000; fax (615)401-2707

BMI's internet address is: www.bmi.com. BMI can
also be reached via e-mail at: losangeles@bmi.com,
nashville@bmi.com and newyork@bmi.com.

ASCAP and BMI also have offices in Atlanta, Miami
London and Puerto Rico. ASCAP also has an office
in Chicago.

2. If your company is not a corporation using its corporate name, in most states it must file a document with the county recorder in which the publishing company is located stating, among other things, the business name that you are operating under. The exact name of the document and the specific requirements vary from state to state, but your county recorder should be able to guide you through your state's particular maze.

In California, the document is called the Fictitious Business Name Statement ("FBNS"). The FBNS must not only be filed with the county recorder's office, but must also appear in a newspaper of general circulation. Your county recorder can tell you which newspapers are acceptable and, based on circulation, which is probably the least expensive.

3. Register the songs with the Copyright Office in Washington, D.C., in the name of your publishing entity. If you have previously registered the songs, file an assignment transferring the copyright ownership of the songs to the publishing entity.

♪ ♪ ♪

Well, it's time for a break. The following pages contain THE "BIG PICTURE" ROYALTY CHART which summarizes the largest royalty payments to artists and songwriters.

THE "BIG PICTURE"

ARTIST'S LARGEST ROYALTIES

Record Royalties:

From record sales. Paid by the record company to the artist in exchange for allowing the record company to make a record featuring the artist.

The amount paid is typically a percentage of the suggested retail list price (SRLP) of the record, less many deductions.

Other Royalties:

From film/TV, advertisement, internet and C D - R O M / D V D master license fees. Paid by film companies, television production companies, internet companies and many others to the record company for the right to use the record company's master recording of the artist's version of the song.

The record company pays the artist his or her share of the fees as agreed to in the record contract.

ROYALTY CHART

SONGWRITER'S LARGEST ROYALTIES

Mechanical Royalties:

From record sales. Paid by a record company to the publisher for the right to include the songwriter's song on a record. The publisher pays the songwriter his or her share.

The publisher receives 100% of this royalty, which is divided into two equal parts (50/50) called (1)the *writer's share*, and (2)the *publisher's share*.

The publisher pays the songwriter the entire *writer's share*.

The publisher pays the songwriter any part of the *publisher's share* retained by the songwriter in the agreement between the songwriter and publisher.

Performing Royalties:

From airplay. Paid by broadcasters such as radio stations, television stations, web broadcasters and other public performance users of a song.

This royalty is divided into two equal parts (50/50) called (1)the *writer's share*, and (2)the *publisher's share*. Monies are paid to ASCAP/BMI/SESAC.

These "performance rights societies" pay the songwriter directly the entire *writer's share*. The society pays the publisher the *publisher's share*. If part of the *publisher's share* is retained by the songwriter, the publisher pays the songwriter that part of the *publisher's share*.

Other Royalties:

From sheet music sales, film/TV, advertisement, internet and CD-ROM/DVD sync license fees. Paid by sheet music companies, film companies, television production companies, internet companies and many others to the publisher for the right to use a song.

The publisher receives 100% of this royalty from the use of the song and, in turn, pays the songwriter his or her share in the same manner that mechanical royalties are paid to the songwriter.

OTHER IMPORTANT BASICS

17. ISSUES BETWEEN BAND MEMBERS

This is one of the least favorite things for band members to discuss. When you are just starting out, everything is great because it's all about the music. The individual members do not have divergent interests. Strong artistic differences haven't surfaced, and there is no money at stake to fight over. Issues between band members, however, must be discussed.

Apart from enjoying the music, make sure that you really like being with the other members of your band. If you are successful, you will be touring together, promoting your band together, and generally spending lots and lots of time together.

Not only does spending a great deal of time with people you don't like become old very quickly, but like it or not, *you will also be in business with them.*

Life is too short for the nightmares that follow when the inevitable disagreements about money surface. If you haven't "made it" yet, you won't think it's an issue, but it will be. When band members do not like each other, money fights can become very nasty.

When a band is just forming, you cannot anticipate or protect against all of the things that may happen, and until you truly believe that the band is going somewhere, it doesn't make sense to spend a lot of money on a lawyer. But, once you believe the band is going to be together for a while, it makes sense to hire a lawyer and have him or her draw up an internal band contract, be it in the form of a partnership, a corporation or a limited liability company.

A good contract between band members will address critical issues including the following:

1. Who owns the band's name in the event of a breakup?
2. Who gets what percentages of profits?
3. How are artistic decisions made if there is a disagreement?
4. Who controls the band's business decisions such as when to tour or firing other band members? and,
5. What happens to a former member's interest if he or she quits or is fired?

If you are the "Pete Best" of the group (the Beatles' drummer before Ringo Starr), waiting until a major-label record deal is at hand to address these questions may be too late. It's better to find out early on where everybody stands.

Another critical question that band members must address is who owns what songwriting and publishing interests. Does each member own the individual copyright to the songs he or she wrote, or does the band own the copyrights to all the band's songs? How about something in the middle (e.g., the person who actually wrote the song owns a bit more of the song)? And, what happens to the copyrights if the band later breaks up?

If, for example, each band member individually owns the

copyrights to their respective songs, the band may be in for a fight when the members try to agree on which song is going to become the album's single; the song with all the airplay. As you will recall from earlier chapters, a band (as artists) can be losing money even though at the same time, the person writing the songs for the band is making a great deal of money. It is easy for the band to come apart when most of the band is still struggling financially, but the songwriting member is living in a new home in Beverly Hills.

So what happens if the band does not have a written contract? The band is treated as a legal partnership. And like a partnership, when one of the band members (i.e., one of the partners) leaves the band, for whatever reason, then legally that partnership terminates automatically.

Of course, the remaining members of the band are free to form a new band, but legally they may not be free to use the old band's name without paying the departing member for the privilege of doing so. This is because without a written contract, the law generally presumes that each band member owns an equal share of the band's physical assets (e.g., the equipment) and intangible assets (e.g., the band's name and logo). Each member of the band is also presumed to (1)share equally in the band's profits and losses, and (2)have an equal vote in the band's affairs. Majority rules!

Quite apart from issues centering around the band's formation and demise are terms of the band's record deal itself, which may leave a band member's ego bruised. Provisions in record contracts must be spelled out. Is the record company going to treat one member as more valuable than the rest? If one member refuses to record, are all the members in breach of the contract? If one member leaves the group, does the record company have the right to void the record deal? Who is responsible to the record company if the band is still "in the red" when one member leaves the band?

A good contract between band members will address the rights and obligations of each individual member. Work out the details with your attorney before you get too big, or you may be in for some ugly legal fights down the road.

18. TRADEMARKS AND SERVICE MARKS

Your band name and logo as a band are potentially valuable assets. You can cripple your future earning power before your career even begins if you don't have an identity that is your own and can't be used by others.

Often, people use the term "copyright" when they really mean "trademark" or "service mark." Basically, the difference is that copyrights protect the expression of artistic ideas (e.g., a songwriter's songs), and trademarks/service marks protect the identifying symbols associated with a particular product or service (e.g., a brand name or a logo).[54]

More specifically, a *trademark* is a word, phrase, symbol or design,[55] which identifies you as the source of goods, and distinguishes you from others offering similar goods. A *service mark* is the same thing except that it identifies and distinguishes you as the source of a service.

Your band's name is used to identify services offered (i.e., the performance of your music), and therefore, is considered a service mark.[56]

---

[54] Copyrights are discussed more fully in Chapter 10.

[55] Or a combination of these. Sounds and colors can also qualify as marks.

[56] Note, however, that when you are offering merchandise for sale with the band's name on it (e.g., T-shirts or mugs), the same mark (i.e., your band's name) can be used as a trademark.

In the United States, when two bands are fighting over a band name which does not infringe on anyone else's service mark or trademark, the right to use the particular band name generally belongs to the band which first uses the name in commerce.[57] A service mark is considered used when the service mark is included in advertising or other promotional material and the service is actually being provided (e.g., your band is a real playing band). Incidentally, the name is not owned by the person in the band who thought it up, but rather by who uses the name (i.e., the band). If a particular member of the band wants to own the band's name, this can be set up through an internal band contract.

Watch out for managers who attempt to control the band's name. I know of a popular band from the sixties and seventies which still occasionally tours together "underground" because they fear the legal wrath of their former manager who owns the right to use the name. Not too long ago, 'N Sync had to settle a huge lawsuit with the manager who started their career so they could keep using their name. If the members of 'N Sync had to tour without their name, would anyone know to come?

Before picking a band name that you truly are attached to and want to keep throughout your career, here are two important suggestions:

---

[57] There are two main exceptions to this: (1)Before you actually began to use the mark, another band filed an application with the U.S. Patent and Trademark Office stating that they intend to use the mark, and the other band's mark later matures to registration; (2)another band files an application for a mark with the U.S. Patent and Trademark Office which is based on a valid foreign mark that they filed before you began using the mark, and is filed within six months of the filing of their original foreign application. If their mark matures to registration, the foreign band's mark will have priority over yours.

1. Do a search of potentially conflicting marks first.
When you hit it big, you don't want someone suing you because
they were using the name before you were. Even if their name is
not actually the same as yours, you could still find yourself
prevented from using your chosen name.

The key legal test of whether a band name infringes on
someone else's service mark or trademark is the "*likelihood of
confusion*" but, as with a growing number of legal issues today,
there is no specific definition of what constitutes a likelihood of
confusion. Rather, there are a number of factors which come
into play and are used by courts to determine the likelihood of
confusion. These include the similarity in the overall impression
created by the two marks, the similarities of the goods and
services involved, and evidence of actual confusion by consumers.

The best way to make sure that your name will be afforded
mark protection (even though no method is foolproof) is to hire
a professional search company to search the records of the U.S.
Patent and Trademark Office ("PTO"), all fifty states, and to also
locate unregistered marks. This will cost several hundred dollars.
Two well respected firms are Corsearch; tel. (800) 732-7241;
web address: www.corsearch.com, and Thomson & Thomson;
tel. (800) 692-8833; web address: www.thomson-thomson.com.

If you cannot afford to hire a professional search firm, at
least make an effort to check trade sources such as:(1)the
American Federation of Musicians, whose offices will tell you
whether they have an exclusive agency contract with a group
that already is using the name you want; tel. (212) 869-1330 in
New York, or (323) 461-3441 in California; internet address:
www.afm.org; (2)*Billboard's International Talent & Touring
Directory* or *The Yellow Pages of Rock*, which list most of the

groups that are actively performing; (3)the web sites of ASCAP, BMI and SESAC and (4)record stores. Also, for federally registered marks only, and *not* for marks registered with a particular state, the PTO also has a search mechanism at its web site. The internet address for the PTO is www.uspto.gov.

2. Make the name of your band distinctive. After you have been using your mark, this will increase your ability to prevent others from using a mark that may create confusion with your mark.[58]

♪ ♪ ♪

Even though trademark and service mark rights are generally created by use, and not by registration with either the PTO or the individual state's Secretary of State, it is a good idea when you start becoming successful to register the name of your band with the PTO.[59] To do so, you must first engage in, or anticipate engaging in, interstate commerce (e.g., playing in another state, selling CDs in another state, or offering for sale a CD via an internet site with reach beyond your home state). By registering your mark, if anyone infringes on it by using a conflicting mark, you will have access to courts and will be able

---

[58] Note that theoretically, a service mark or trademark cannot be registered if it consists of "immoral matter."

[59] Of course, it is more prudent to register your mark before you begin using it, but, as I will discuss shortly, it can be quite costly to do so. If you see the symbol ® at the end of a mark, it means that the mark has been federally registered with the PTO. Incidentally, the symbols TM and SM that you have probably come across are unofficial and are used only to give notice to others that you claim trademark (TM) or service mark (SM) ownership in an unregistered mark. You can use these liberally if you wish. Because people are afraid that it will make their 'art' seem commercial, TM and SM do not seem to be used often in the entertainment industry.

to obtain an injunction to stop them.[60]

You can reach the PTO at its web site or as follows: U.S. Department of Commerce/Patent and Trademark Office, Washington, D.C. 20231; tel. (800) 786-9199. When you file an application to register a mark, the PTO first looks for other marks that may be the same as, or similar to, yours. Then, if they find the application to be clear of conflicting marks, they publish your proposed mark in the *U.S. Official Gazette* so that others can look at your mark and raise objections, if they have any. It usually takes over a year to obtain the registration even if everything goes perfectly and no one has any objection to the registration of your mark.

Proper registration of a mark can cost thousands of dollars. This is because the PTO classifies different goods and services in forty two separate *"classes,"* and a separate fee is charged to register a mark in each class. For example, to register your band's name as performers of music (class 41) is different than registering your band's name for use on T-shirts (class 25). In addition, fees paid to the PTO do not include your attorneys' fees, which will be a minimum of several hundred dollars, assuming everything goes smoothly.

I strongly suggest that you do not attempt to register your mark without enlisting the help of an attorney who specializes in trademark law. The importance of properly protecting your mark is great, and there are simply too many ways to leave yourself exposed.

---

[60] Note however, that at present, your band is not afforded any service mark or trademark protection from merely obtaining its own internet domain name. You must also show an actual use in commerce.

19. ON TOUR

Touring occurs year round, but the major touring season occurs during the summer months. No one except major stars makes any real money touring. For everyone else, touring is done primarily to help promote record sales.

The contracts used for tours booked by music agents are customarily AFM standard printed forms. The real "guts" of such tour agreements, however, are attached to the form. The attachment is called a "rider" to the contract, and it can be over 25 pages long. Important items of negotiation include limiting promoter expenses, merchandising, and technical specifications such as an artist's equipment, lighting and stage setup requirements.

If, for any reason, you (as an artist or a band) are booking your own tours, always make sure you have a written contract signed by the club owner *before* you show up to perform at a club. Many times the dates of performance, compensation, and the sound equipment to be provided get screwed up if an artist does not have a written contract.

New artists should not tour until their record is out. If you just made your own CD and are getting only a little airplay on college radio, don't expect any club to pay you more than a few hundred dollars a night. More than likely, they will give you a percentage of the gross proceeds from ticket sales. The percentage may be as high as 65% or so, but may be a lot lower if other artists are playing there that night as well.

If an artist's record is beginning to sell well, the artist can get paid $1,000 to $15,000 a night for headlining at a large club, and up to $15,000 or $20,000 for opening for a major act at an amphitheater or stadium. This may sound like pretty good money, but in many cases the artist will agree to a significantly reduced payment, especially if he or she wants exposure to the headliner's audience. And oftentimes, when headlining at a club, the contract still calls for the artist to receive a percentage of the gross proceeds from ticket sales. In the final analysis, an artist must compare the gross income received to the actual expense of going on tour.

It can *easily* cost $10,000 or more to "economically" put a band on the road for a week without the members drawing any salary (you must pay for food and lodging, equipment rental, truck or bus rental, a minimal crew, insurance, and commissions to agents and managers). An artist or a band can lose a lot of money by going on tour! Sometimes, money may be advanced by the record company as "tour support" because the record company wants the artist out there selling records.

A moderately successful artist (i.e., 200,000 to 500,000 album sales) may be able to make a bit on tours, but they can lose a lot of money as well. He or she can headline in 2000-seat venues and get paid $10,000 or more per night, but, unless their fans are willing to pay $20 to $25 or more for the show, the primary business purpose of the tour is still to sell records.

Major stars do make money on tours even though the costs can be astronomical. On Cher's last tour, she took six 18-wheelers, and four busses to transport her people and props. On a recent Janet Jackson extravaganza, she had one bus just for security guards, and another bus just for shoes! Major stars get paid minimum guarantees (up to several hundred thousand dollars per night) against a percentage of net profits of the show (85% is typical; 90% if the artist is willing to forgo the guarantee). The promoter keeps the rest.

Like the rest of the maturing music business, there is a great consolidation in ownership and control of the top venues of the touring business. Currently, one company, Clear Channel Communications, through its subsidiary SFX Entertainment, owns or operates over 80% of the large amphitheaters in the U.S.

20. SELLING MERCHANDISE

Once you have your record deal and publishing deal in place, you will have plenty of advisors to protect you with regard to merchandising.

If you are just starting out, you are probably selling your own CDs, silk-screened T-shirts and caps at your shows. I do not mean to scare you (and as long as you are relatively small no one may care very much), but be aware that when you sell merchandise, there are rules. There are city taxes, state taxes, business license fees and other local fees that must be paid. If you have a "roadie" or a friend doing the selling for you, they may technically be an "employee" of yours and payroll taxes must be paid. In any event, you probably won't be making a lot of money from merchandise sales until you hit the big time.

With rare exceptions, during a tour of a successful artist, the artist will license the right to use his or her name and likeness to a merchandiser. There are a surprising number of bidding wars that serve to increase artist advances and guarantees. Three larger tour merchandisers are Winterland, Signatures Network (affiliated with Sony) and Giant (affiliated with WEA). The royalty paid to the artist is generally 28% to 33% of the gross sales of the merchandise. Major stars can receive 40% or more of the gross, or 90% of the net profits. Generally, gross sales of merchandise of adult-oriented groups (e.g., Rolling Stones, Sting, etc.) can average $5 per person at the concert. Heavy metal groups can sell $7-$8 of merchandise per person. Hot touring acts, such as Backstreet Boys or 'N Sync, may sell $12 of merchandise per person. The average sales per person does go down at larger venues.

Keep your image in mind. You don't want "schlock" out there with your name on it. Items of negotiation with a merchandising company include; the amount of advances to the artist, creative control over the merchandise, the merchandiser's exclusive right to market, performance guarantees (i.e., that the artist or band will show up and play before a given number of people during the tour), and sell-off rights of excess merchandise at the end of the tour.

For merchandise sold at places other than concerts, the royalties paid by merchandisers to the artist for the right to manufacture the goods (or sub-license someone else to do so in the U.S.) are generally a lot less. One night of sales at a major concert can net the artist more than a full year of nationwide retail sales. Typically, royalties for clothing (mostly T-shirts and caps) sold at traditional retail outlets are 10% to 12-1/2% of the retail sales price, while royalties for other items (such as bumper stickers, buttons and posters) are 8% to 10% of the sales price. Sales over the internet generally result in royalties of 15%-25% of the retail sale price.

21. A LITTLE ABOUT MUSIC VIDEOS

Back in 1983, the trade magazine *Billboard* estimated that consistent exposure on MTV was boosting record sales by 15% to 20%. This started a boom. Flash forward to the 21st century and music videos are on television everywhere. They are also soon to be all over the internet. Today, many music buyers find out about new music from television and multi-media sources, not radio. Visual media's influence on the music scene is greater than ever.

Typically, the cost of making a professional video is $60,000 to $100,000 for a new or moderately successful artist, $100,000 to $250,000 or even higher for a major star. Unless you are signed to a label and have national distribution of your record in place, forget the idea of having MTV or VH1 play your video.

You can, however, make a decent video for under $15,000 and have it played on local television, or available for play on the internet. Even at this reduced cost, however, it still may not be a good use of your funds, when you compare it to other methods of promotion. If you feel you must make a video, here are a few budget-saving tips that have been passed on to me from people familiar with production:

1. Use exterior daylight or minimal lighting.
2. Forget dance numbers.
3. Put your money into editing the video and syncing the music to it; rely on favors for rehearsal space, for getting the best video and sound equipment you can, and for the video shoot itself.

MUSIC, MOTION PICTURES, TELEVISION & MULTI-MEDIA

This topic really requires a book of its own, and will probably not be too important to an artist or songwriter who is not already signed to a record or publishing deal, or is not a good friend of one of the following: a movie/television music coordinator, a big shot with an internet company in need of music, a CD-ROM or DVD producer, or an executive with an advertising music supplier. Nevertheless, the following pages contain some highlights.

Remember, there is no compulsory license that allows film companies, television production companies, CD-ROM or DVD makers, most internet users, or advertising agencies to use your song or your performance of a song without permission. Therefore, the fees are negotiable and highly volatile.

22. THEATRICAL MOTION PICTURES

In order to obtain the rights to use even one performance of a song as part of a motion picture, a film company may need to enter into many separate contracts. The film company may need to make deals with the performing artist, the songwriter (and publisher), the record company of the performer (both to use existing masters and clearing the right to use the record company's exclusive artist on the film soundtrack album), and finally, with the record company that is going to make the film soundtrack album.

There are essentially three categories of music that may be part of a motion picture: (1)songs which are specifically written to be an integral part of a motion picture (e.g., "My Heart Will Go On" in the movie *Titanic*); (2)songs which were not originally written for the film but are used in the film (e.g., "Hound Dog" in the movie *Forrest Gump*; and (3)the background music you hear throughout a film while actors are conversing and action is taking place (this is the movie's "score," also known as the "underscore").

1) SONGS SPECIFICALLY WRITTEN FOR A PARTICULAR MOTION PICTURE

Before the artist or songwriter can make a deal with the film company, both must make sure that they are allowed to do so under the terms of their record contract and publishing contract, respectively.[61]

The Artist

For a song specifically written for a particular motion picture, the artist receives a flat fee (for the performance itself) and royalties (if a movie soundtrack album is made).[62] The amount of the fee can be all over the board and depends mostly on who needs who. A major artist may receive as much as $500,000 up front. A falling star in need of publicity, by contrast, may perform a song for as little as minimum union scale if the film is right. The total royalty paid on the soundtrack album (divided by all of the artists appearing on the album) is usually 12% to 15% of the SRLP. This percentage can, of course, be higher if one of the artists is a major star. Typically, an artist's record company will want to keep 50% of their artist's royalties (for letting the artist out of their "exclusive" arrangement) if the soundtrack album is released by another record company.

The Songwriter

Typically, a songwriter is hired to write a song for a movie as a "work for hire." The songwriter's payment is a flat fee plus songwriter royalties. The fee can range anywhere from $0 to $35,000, depending on how established the songwriter is and how important the film company believes the song will be to the movie. Generally, however, film companies almost never obligate themselves to use a particular song, although with an established

---

[61] Major artists who write their own songs often negotiate "package deals" with film and television production companies, whereby the artist/songwriter receives one up-front fee and a combination of royalties which, in effect, merges the royalties earned from being both the artist and the songwriter.

[62] Royalty payments may also be earned from foreign distribution of the film.

songwriter, they will usually agree to pay for the song whether they ultimately use it or not. Film companies also enter into "step" deals — where a film company pays the songwriter a small amount initially to make the demo, and then more later if the film company ultimately decides to use the song. Often, intermediate payments between the initial demo and ultimate completion of a song (i.e., "step" payments) are tied to refinements of the song made by the songwriter at the film company's request.

Even in the typical case, in which the song is written as a "work for hire," the songwriter's royalties are the same as those for any other ordinary songwriter deal.[63] Also, if the songwriter is well-established, the songwriter may retain a portion of the *publisher's share* of the song. The reason film companies usually insist on hiring the songwriter on a "work for hire" basis, is so that the songwriter will not be allowed to reclaim full copyright ownership after 35 years.[64]

2) SONGS WHICH WERE NOT ORIGINALLY WRITTEN FOR A FILM BUT ARE LATER USED IN A FILM

For songs which were not originally written for a particular film, but are later used in that film, the film company has to acquire a license from the songwriter's publisher and may also require a license from the artist's record company. Here is how the artist and songwriter get paid:

---

[63] See Chapter 12, "Primary Sources of Income," Chapter 13, "Secondary Sources of Income," and Chapter 14, "Music Publishing."

[64] See footnote 51.

The Artist

If the film company wants to use a particular version of a song that is already on a record, the film company must obtain a *master recording license* from the record company. This gives the film company the right to use the record company's master recording. The artist typically receives 50% of the license royalty (i.e., whatever percentage is in the artist-record company contract). The license royalty fees charged by record companies can range from $10,000 to $100,000. If the deal calls for granting the film company rights to make a soundtrack album, the film company will pay an additional royalty of 12% to 15% of the SRLP. Typically, the artist's record company will retain half of these royalties and the artist will receive the other half.

The Songwriter

In many films, a new recording of a popular song is made by an artist, thereby avoiding any requirement to obtain a master recording license from a particular record company. A major artist may receive as much as $500,000 up front to record the song. But, whether or not the film company wishes to use a record company's master recording, the film company must still negotiate with the copyright owner of the song (i.e., the publisher) to obtain a *sync license*, giving them the right to use the musical composition. Without the sync license, the *no* version of the song can be used. Synchronization fees for publishing are often similar to those paid to the record company for use of the master recording ($10,000 to $100,000).

3) THE BACKGROUND SCORE

For writing the score of a major film, the composer will

receive a fee ranging from $30,000 to $700,000 (unless you are John Williams or James Horner, in which case the fee is closer to $1,000,000). In addition to songwriter royalties, the composer, like any artist, may also receive a royalty payment for each record sold (7% to 10% of the SRLP). Additionally, if the composer produces the recordings, he or she will receive an additional producer's royalty (3% to 4% of the SRLP).

With the necessary use licenses in hand, the film company is free to strike a deal with any record/distribution company to put out a soundtrack album. Often, all three categories of music discussed above are a part of the same film and will be included in varying degrees on the soundtrack album. If only some of the music on a soundtrack album is expected to be the catalyst that generates the sales, the amount of royalties different people and entities are to receive from that soundtrack album will be heavily contested.

23. TELEVISION

The licenses that must be obtained for use of a song in television shows and made-for-TV movies are the same as those for theatrical motion pictures. There are some differences between the two mediums, however. First, unlike songs used in theatrical motion pictures shown in U.S. theaters, the songwriter will receive performing royalties (i.e., ASCAP/BMI payments) from songs used on television. Second, in part because payments are received from ASCAP/BMI, and in part because the exposure from television is much greater than that of film, payments to the artist and songwriter for songs used in television are much smaller. The exposure helps trigger an increase in the other sources of income from a song.

As with motion pictures, there are essentially three categories of music that may be part of a television program: (1)songs specifically written for a particular television program; (2)songs which were not originally written for a particular program but are later used in one; and (3)the television background score.

1) SONGS WRITTEN SPECIFICALLY FOR A PARTICULAR TELEVISION PROGRAM

There are not many songs written specifically for a particular television program other than the theme song. Since some television theme songs are composed by the show's background composers, for an additional fee, these songs are often included as part of the initial background composing contract. This contract will generally state that all of the songs written by the composer for the television program are "works for hire."

2) SONGS WHICH WERE NOT ORIGINALLY WRITTEN FOR A PARTICULAR TELEVISION PROGRAM BUT ARE LATER USED IN ONE

With regard to the use of preexisting songs in a television show, the producer must secure the rights to use such songs from the publishers who own them. The usual sync licensing fees charged by publishers range from $500 to $1,800 for a license authorizing use of a song in a television program or series for worldwide perpetual distribution, but on occasion the sync fee can be as high as $10,000. If a well-known song is going to be used as the theme song for a television program, the publisher may charge the television production company anywhere from $1,500 to $10,000 per episode.

In addition to the sync license, if the producer wishes to use a particular version of the song that is on a record, a separate master recording license must be obtained from the record company. This is like free advertising for future sales of the record company's record, and so the fees charged are low.

3) THE BACKGROUND SCORE

The background score constitutes the vast majority of the music heard on television. Such creative fees can range from $3,500 to $9,000 per episode ($10,000 to $30,000 for a package of multiple episodes), depending on such factors as how established the composer is, the length of the program being written for, and the size of the music budget. As with other music composed for movies and television, the standard television background composing contract states that the composer's music is a "work for hire." Therefore, the composer does not retain ownership of the copyright. The composer may, however, retain an interest in the royalties earned by the background score.

In a properly negotiated contract, when an American television program or made-for-TV movie is re-released in foreign movie theaters or on pay television in the U.S. (e.g., Cinemax, HBO), an additional fee will be paid to the artist and/or songwriter. Also, an additional fee is paid if the television program or movie is distributed for home video use.

24. CD-ROM AND DVD

As in motion pictures and television, if anyone wants to include a performance of a song on their CD-ROM or DVD, they may need to make separate deals with the performing artist, the songwriter (through the publisher), and the record company of the performer (both to use existing masters and to clear the right to use the record company's exclusive artist on the CD-ROM or DVD). Again, as with film and TV, the artist will receive payment (through his or her record company) for use of the master recording, and the songwriter will receive payment (through his or her publisher) for use of the song.

The types of deals being made, and the dollar amounts involved, are all over the board and quite fluid. Some deals do generate a flat fee of hundreds of thousands of dollars, while others generate a set number of pennies per each unit sold. Some deals have in-kind promotion or marketing tie-ins as part of the deal (e.g., when you advertise the CD-ROM game, you have to mention the name of our band, and by the way, we get the right to approve the way you use our name).

Here are some of the factors that lead to a higher or lower price: (1)the anticipated unit sales of the specific CD-ROM or DVD; (2)the amount of the song or record used on the CD-ROM or DVD; (3)the commercial appeal of the artist; (4)the popularity of the song or record; and (5)the perceived importance of the song or record to the success of the CD-ROM or DVD.

As an artist, make sure your record deal calls for you to receive 50% of the income (the same royalty you receive from income generated from film) generated from CD-ROM, DVD and other yet-to-be-invented multi-media formats. As a songwriter, make sure that your publishing deal (even if you own part of the publishing) calls for you to receive the full songwriter's share of income generated from CD-ROM, DVD and other yet-to-be-invented multi-media formats.

25. THE INTERNET

Everything that applies to CD-ROM and DVD deals applies to internet deals, only in spades.[65] The internet is completely fragmented. Therefore, it is extremely difficult to determine the appropriate fee that should be paid for using a particular song or performance.

Clearly the appropriate fee which can be charged to a small business which desires to use a musical clip, or to a person who desires to use their favorite song on a personal web page, is much different from the fee which can be charged to the host company of a web site with millions of visitors daily. The business structure for what is appropriate to charge isn't in place because the internet is still in its infancy, and we have already seen one boom and bust cycle.

In 2002, new law effectively mandated that certain web-casters (e.g., commercial internet radio stations) pay set royalty rates to owners of master recordings.[66] Not surprisingly, these rates are deemed to be too low by record companies and artists, and much too high by small internet radio stations who have listeners, but no profits. Legal challenges, and pleas to Congress are still ongoing.

---

[65] Note that I'm not talking about sales of CDs via the internet or downloads of music to ipods and the like. The royalty rates from these sales are set in your record contract or your publishing deal. The fact that a record is sold via the internet rather than through a traditional retailer doesn't affect your royalty rate unless your record or publishing deal says it does.

Because technology, economic models and the copyright law associated with the internet are quite fluid, the important thing as an artist, is to make sure that your record deal calls for you to receive 50% of the income generated from licensing music to internet sites (the same royalty you receive from income generated from film). As a songwriter, make sure that your publishing deal (even if you own part of the publishing) calls for you, as the songwriter, to receive the full songwriter's share of income generated from licensing music to internet sites.[67]

---

[66] The Recording Industry Association of America website, www.riaa.com, contains an excellent Webcasting FAQ section which specifies the webcasters covered and gives the applicable rates.

[67] Broadcasts on the internet also entitle the songwriter and publisher to performing rights payments through ASCAP, BMI or SESAC. These payments, while still small, will grow over time. The songwriter's share of this payment will be paid to the songwriter directly from the performing rights society, not from the publisher. In addition, it is legally uncertain when and if mechanical royalties should be paid to the copyright owner of the song itself.

26. JINGLES

Jingles are songs used primarily for advertising on television and radio. In order to get your song used as a jingle, you will have to have an "in" with an advertising agency, an advertising music supplier (e.g., a "jingle house" representing many composers), or a producer producing such music. There are essentially two types of songs used as jingles: (1)songs written for a specific advertising campaign, and (2)existing songs.

1) SONGS WRITTEN FOR A SPECIFIC AD CAMPAIGN

After an advertising campaign is selected by a company and its ad agency, a music supplier is hired to provide the music for the jingle if the agency does not write the music in-house. The music supplier may be an independent writer or a jingle production company which is typically owned by a writer. The ad agency customarily provides the lyrics for the jingle. The amount charged by the music supplier is two-fold: (1)a creative fee (typically ranging from $7,500 to as much as $25,000 for one 30-second commercial; but if the advertising campaign involves a major celebrity artist/songwriter, the creative fees may be in the millions); and (2)production costs (to cover the costs of hiring musicians and studio rental).

The music supplier provides the finished master and often writes the music as well. Therefore, the music supplier, as a musician, is entitled to residual royalty payments per AFM, SAG or AFTRA union contracts. In addition, music suppliers, as composers and publishers, may receive a small amount of performing royalties from ASCAP/BMI.[68]

2) EXISTING SONGS

If an ad agency wishes to use a particular version of a song that is already on a record, they must acquire the rights to use the song by (1)obtaining a master use license from the record company, *and* (2)obtaining a sync license from the songwriter's publisher.[69] License fees vary greatly, depending on such factors as whether the song is to be played on television or radio, the length of the song's use, the song's popularity, whether the use of the song is limited to certain types of products, and how elaborate the arrangement is. For a national commercial, the going rate an advertiser must pay to obtain a master use license and sync license of a popular song ranges from $50,000 to well over $1,000,000. As an example of what advertisers are willing to pay to use the right song in an advertisement, AT&T paid over $1,000,000 to merely use the instrumental portion of Madonna's song "Ray of Light."

---

[68] If an ad agency wishes to save money, e.g., for a low-budget ad campaign, they may license existing stock music (usually background scores) from a music library or a post-production house. The license fees for such music are generally very low (e.g., less than $100), with no residuals payable to the songwriters. Such music is usually recorded in nonunion sessions abroad.

[69] The ad agency need not obtain a master use license if it re-records a new version of the song; rather, only a sync license is necessary.

CONCLUSION

Congratulations! You've made it through a lot of difficult information about the deal points and numbers that guide the music business. If I've done my job, you now have a better understanding of the music business and are much less likely to get ripped off.

Even if everything I've discussed didn't sink in the first time you read it, it is my hope that you will refer to this book time and time again as a guide to alert you to any "red flags" suggesting that someone might be trying to take advantage of you. Use it to ask questions of lawyers, record company personnel and anyone else in the business you come in contact with. If someone asks you to sign a contract or give up rights that don't seem to line up with the suggested deal points or numbers in this book, don't just sign on the dotted line — call them on it.

Good luck with your music career.

I have compiled this book as an educational tool. Because of the constantly changing laws related to this field, the information presented in this book should not be construed as legal advice, but merely educational information. For advice on any specific question, please contact an attorney.

APPENDIX I -- CONTRACTS

Most people don't seem to know exactly what a contract is, when they've entered into a binding one (unless they've signed something with very small print), or what they've actually agreed to do when they have signed something (too much legalese). That is why I have included this appendix.

What Is A Contract?

A contract, any contract, is simply a voluntary agreement between people to trade anything of value (for example — money, possessions, or your services). That's it. If you have an agreement, you have a contract.

A contract can go by any number of different names; it doesn't have to be called a contract to be one. Here are just a few other names for a contract: deal... agreement... arrangement... understanding... and even sometimes, "but you promised."

If a friend of yours says, I'll sell you my guitar for $500 dollars, it becomes a contract once you say OK... deal... you got it... or anything else indicating that your friend's offer to sell you his guitar is accepted. Like most contracts in the U.S. that can be performed in less than one year, it doesn't have to be in writing to be binding on both of you.[70]

---

[70] Some contracts do need to be in writing even if they can be performed in under one year. For instance, transfers of copyright ownership (§204 of the Copyright Act); and in California, where I am an attorney, personal services contracts, such as publishing and record deals, to the extent that an injunction might be sought to stop you from recording for another company (Cal. Civil Code §3423); certain real estate deals and wills (Cal. Civil Code §1624).

Because a contract exists, if you or your friend don't do what you agreed to do, then the other can sue to enforce the contract.

Reasons Contracts Are Put In Writing

There are two main reasons contracts are usually put in writing (apart from when required by law): First, the process of putting a contract in writing makes it less likely that there will be a misunderstanding about what was agreed to (i.e., someone saying, "but I never agreed to that"). For example, what if you thought you were buying your friend's exquisite Martin guitar, but your friend thought he was selling you his Ibenez knock-off? In that case, you two never agreed to anything, and no contract was formed. You didn't have what the law calls the *"meeting-of-the-minds."*

The other reason to put a contract in writing is that by doing so, it makes it easier to prove in court what the terms of the contract are. If a written contract said your friend would sell you his Martin, it would be hard for him to argue in front of a judge or jury that the agreement called for selling you the Ibenez.

There Is No Such Thing As A Standard Contract

There is no such thing as a standard written contract that cannot be changed. If someone tells you something is standard, my advice is to ignore them. Remember this when a publisher or record company tells you that this is their standard contract and it can't be changed. This is just a method of negotiation.

If You Don't Understand It, Don't Sign It

When you enter into a contract make sure you understand what you are signing. Substitute English and minimize the legalese wherever you can. Legalese impresses lawyers and insecure muckamucks. The words "in the event that" is just a fancy way to say "if"; "the party of the first part" is just a ridiculous way of saying a person's name. It made sense in your great grandparents' time, an era that had no word processing and no copy machines. It doesn't make sense now. Everyone who signs a contract should understand what they are signing. By doing so, disputes will be kept to a minimum. If there is a lawsuit somewhere down the road, a judge or jury will more likely understand the plain meaning of the agreement without the other side's lawyer being able to twist its meaning.

Use Riders Or Addendums

Sometimes it's easier in negotiation to add something to the end of someone else's contract rather than changing the contract form itself. Some people hate the thought of anyone messing with their form, but don't seem to mind if someone adds to it. If handled the right way, an addition wipes out what is said in their form contract anyway. The addition at the end of a contract is often called a rider or an addendum (but you can call it anything you like). In a rider, make sure to start by saying something like, "To the extent that the terms contained in this Rider are in conflict with the main text of the Contract, the terms of this Rider control and govern." By including this type of language, if the rider says one thing, and the main text of the contract says something that contradicts it, it's as if the main text of the contract says nothing at all.

APPENDIX II -- IMPORTANT INTERNET SITES

With almost certainty, any record label and music publisher you can name has a robust internet site. A couple of clicks through your favorite internet search engine, and you will be transported there. Here are other important and useful sites you may not have thought to visit before you read this book.

Copyright and Trademark Protection --

> **U.S. Copyright Office:**
> http://www.loc.gov/copyright

> **U.S. Patent and Trademark Office:**
> http://www.uspto.gov

Performing Rights Societies --

> **ASCAP:** http://www.ascap.com
> **BMI:** http://www.bmi.com
> **SESAC:** http://www.sesac.com

National Music Publishers Association -- Harry Fox Agency:
> http://www.harryfox.com

Unions --

> **AFM :** http://www.afm.org
> **AFTRA:** http://www.aftra.org

RECOMMENDED READING

I would like to acknowledge other outstanding sources of information (apart from those already listed elsewhere) from which you may benefit:

Avalon, Moses. *Confessions of a Record Producer.* San Francisco, CA: Miller Freeman, 2002.

Brabec, Jeffrey and Brabec, Todd. *Music, Money, and Success.* New York, NY: Schirmer Books, 2002.

Dannen, Fredric. *Hit Men.* New York, NY: Vintage Books, 1991.

Halloran, Mark. *The Musician's Business and Legal Guide.* Englewood Cliffs, NJ: Prentice-Hall, Inc., 2001.

Frascogna, Xavier and Hetherington, H. Lee. *This Business of Artist Management.* New York, NY: Billboard Books, 2003.

Krasilovsky, M. William and Shemel, Sidney. *This Business of Music.* New York, NY: Billboard Books, 2003.

Passman, Donald S. *All You Need To Know About The Music Business.* New York, NY: Simon & Schuster, 2003.

Poe, Randy. *Music Publishing: A Songwriter's Guide.* Cincinnati, OH: Writer's Digest Books, 1997.

Stim, Richard. *Music Law: How To Run Your Band's Business.* Berkeley, CA: Nolo Press, 2003.

If you are thinking of putting out your own record, take a look at:

Schwartz, Dayelle Deanna. *Start and Run Your Own Record Label.* New York, NY: Billboard Books, 2003.

An older but still somewhat useful reference is:

Sweeny, Tim and Geller, Mark. *Guide to Releasing Independent Records.* Torrace, CA: TSA Books, 1996.

ABOUT THE AUTHOR

David Naggar, Esq., is an attorney in San Francisco, California. Mr. Naggar graduated Phi Beta Kappa from the University of California at Berkeley in 1978, where he received a Bachelor of Science degree in Business Administration. He received his Juris Doctor from the University of California, at Berkeley (Boalt Hall) School of Law in 1981. Since graduating from law school, Mr. Naggar has, in addition to practicing law, interned in the Creative Department of the music publishing giant, Warner-Chappell. On the lighter side, Mr. Naggar fancies himself a semi-skilled musician, having played drums professionally for many years.

A NOTE FROM THE AUTHOR

I really want you to actually get through this book and learn from it. That is why I made it concise, rather than 400 pages of typically confusing lawyerese. As with the first edition of this book, I have made every effort to explain what you need to know in plain English. Because I want to give a little back to the music community, I have made sure that the price of this edition has not increased.

Good luck with your music career.